ALTERNATE LIVES

ALTERNATE LIVES

RICHARD AVERY

Copyright © 2025 Richard Avery

The moral right of the author has been asserted.

Apart from any fair dealing for the purposes of research or private study, or criticism or review, as permitted under the Copyright, Designs and Patents Act 1988, this publication may only be reproduced, stored or transmitted, in any form or by any means, with the prior permission in writing of the publishers, or in the case of reprographic reproduction in accordance with the terms of licences issued by the Copyright Licensing Agency. Enquiries concerning reproduction outside those terms should be sent to the publishers.

This is a work of fiction. Names, characters, businesses, places, events and incidents are either the products of the author's imagination or used in a fictitious manner. Any resemblance to actual persons, living or dead, or actual events is purely coincidental.

The manufacturer's authorised representative in the EU for product safety is Authorised Rep Compliance Ltd, 71 Lower Baggot Street, Dublin D02 P593 Ireland
(www.arccompliance.com)

Troubador Publishing Ltd
Unit E2 Airfield Business Park,
Harrison Road, Market Harborough,
Leicestershire LE16 7UL
Tel: 0116 279 2299
Email: books@troubador.co.uk
Web: www.troubador.co.uk

ISBN 978 1 83628 155 9

British Library Cataloguing in Publication Data.
A catalogue record for this book is available from the British Library.

Printed and bound by CPI Group (UK) Ltd, Croydon, CR0 4YY
Typeset in 11pt Minion Pro by Troubador Publishing Ltd, Leicester, UK

To Jane, Daniel, Ruth and Emily, as well as all my relatives, friends, acquaintances, lovers, heroes and villains, both real and imagined. Thank you for your inspiration. I have done my best; I only wish it could have been better.

CONTENTS

Preface	ix
An Old Man Dreaming Dreams	1
A Glance Through the Window	8
Family Secrets	11
The Deep Dark Woods	30
The Girl on the Pink Bicycle	46
A Stormy Night in Georgia	63
Skinny Dipping at the Bishop's	69
Lost Horizons	80
That Most Magical of Fruits	91
Buster	98
The Letter	109
A Tale of Forty-Six	126
Gone	132
A Message from the Past	138
Lives of Quiet Desperation	145
Now and Then	152
The Mallorcan Job	178
The Rise of the Zombie Morris Dancers	194

PREFACE

My life has been fairly uneventful, almost boring one might say, so scared have I been of making any mistakes. Such an existence has, however, given my imagination the opportunity to wander wild and free. Supposing my imagined life became real? Would it work out as I hoped and bring me happiness and delight, or would it instead deliver little beyond misery and distress? However it developed, there is one thing of which I am sure: it would have been different. As Heraclitus the Greek philosopher once wrote: *No man ever steps in the same river twice, for it is not the same river and he is not the same man.*

As I have grown older, I have become obsessed with this thought, wondering how changed my life might have been had I been less afraid and allowed myself to step into other rivers.

Alternate Lives is a collection of eighteen stories selected from over one hundred. Written in the first person, each explores what might have been had I led a different life, whether in personality, body, location or time.

Seventeen of these tales are fictions. However, even they often contain within them at least a smidgen of truth. As George R. R. Martin put it: *The best lies contain within them nuggets of truth, enough to give a listener pause.*

One story, although incomplete, is completely true. Which one? Well, that is for me to know and for you to guess. Enjoy.

AN OLD MAN DREAMING DREAMS

As I sit in my tiny overheated room watching the daily news, it seems that things have changed little in Moscow from my time there nearly sixty years ago. My decision to remain silent for fear of endangering those I once thought of as friends seems to have been the correct one.

Lately, however, my belief in the rightness of that choice has begun to waver. Even though much of my past is lost to me, some memories of those years remain, haunting my dreams with such clarity that my nights are, once more, lost in fear and dread. In the hope that I might regain a little peace, I have decided to reveal to you the details of a single event, one so innocuous that its telling can surely cause no one any harm. This is the tale of Andrei Andreyevich.

*

I shivered. It had been a mistake not to bring my coat. Perhaps I should go back to the office to collect it. And that is what I meant to do, I really did. But then, as I heard that almost imperceptible chime, the tinkling of fracturing glass, a noise you only hear in the middle of a Russian winter, I became distracted. *Shaput zvezda*, I remembered. Literally, the whisper of the stars. The sound one's breath makes when it freezes on contact with the air and falls to earth. I smiled; my Russian was improving. And with that, coat forgotten, I stepped into the night.

The feeble glow from the streetlamps did little to give any relief from the all-pervading gloom. It had been this way all day; a perpetual twilight so dense that I scarcely noticed the transition from morning, past afternoon, towards a night as dark as jet. And through the shadows came the sound of a distant trumpet playing jazz. *Moscow Nights: how appropriate*, I thought.

"Don't use the metro," my boss told me the day I arrived. "You have no idea who will be watching. Get a reliable driver instead. Mine, Dmitry," he continued, "has a cousin who is looking for a client. He has been unemployed since he got out of jail nearly a year ago. He will be cheap."

At first, I argued that I had already explored the metro with its endless escalators, magnificent vaulted ceilings and marbled floors.

"Surely," I said, "it would be far more difficult to observe me there."

Also, the metro ran from nearby Taganskaya and with one change delivered me directly to the end of the street where my apartment lay. So much more convenient for me. But my boss insisted. In the end, my training triumphed and I obeyed.

My doubts only increased the first time I met Andrei Andreyevich.

"My name is Andrei Andreyevich. Call me anything you like as long as it's not late for dinner. Late for dinner; an English joke, you understand?"

Andrei Andreyevich; not the Russian bear I was expecting, more a skinny weasel, the perfect bit-part player in a gangster movie. Stunted and blessed with terminal acne, his Brylcreemed hair shone like a billiard ball as he delivered a heady odour of vodka, cheap tobacco and an absence of soap. His smile, however, was pure eighteen carat.

With few options and not wishing to alienate Dmitry, who seemed to have an unhealthy and mysterious hold over my boss, Andrei Andreyevich and I entered into a simple arrangement. In return for me paying him a full-time salary, he devoted two hours or so a day to meeting my needs – driving me to the office, at a steady fifty kilometres an hour regardless of traffic or weather, and taking me home for the evening, occasionally dropping me at a restaurant of his choosing. At those times, he had an unerring compass for finding establishments that could serve a meal far beyond the customary pleasures of cabbage-and-potato soup.

"Good food, much vodka, plenty pretty girls, this place. It belongs to my cousin," he would explain.

About once a week, if the cooking facilities in my apartment were in operation, he would take me to the hallowed halls of Eliseevsky on Tverskaya. With exquisite chandeliers hanging from its highly decorated ceilings, the vast food halls gave every impression of being a rich man's Harrods. Somehow, Andrei Andreyevich always knew when a delivery of delicacies unavailable to the common folk was due and invariably got me there long before the party locusts descended. At these times, the normally empty but ornately carved shelves were full to overflowing.

When not servicing my needs, Andrei Andreyevich considered the rest of the day his own.

Although we never became close, we learnt to tolerate each other, our journeys always spent in the same way: debating the relative merits of Dynamo versus United, Yashin against Banks, and vodka over single malt. It was the perfect arrangement; me, a make-believe clerk at the British Council, and him, I suspect, a pretend driver. And that is the way of it, I suppose, when everyone is play-acting and living in the shadows.

Regardless, the system mostly worked. Before I needed his services, I telephoned a number, never answered by Andrei Andreyevich himself, and thirty minutes later I walked from the office to find him and his car waiting outside. Except for this one evening. His usual parking space was deserted. Where the hell could he be?

Looking around, I saw him only two or three minutes' walk away. Wrapped in multiple layers topped with a dirty overcoat and the ubiquitous black fur hat, even at a distance Andrei Andreyevich was unmistakable. As the thick dark smoke from his roll-up rose and mingled with the cloying diesel fumes climbing languidly from his car's exhaust, he looked for all the world like a man up to no good. He was engaged in some illicit transaction no doubt, which was why he had parked so far away. As he kept watch, another equally disreputable character moved a series of boxes from his own boot into Andrei Andreyevich's.

Transfer complete, he was passed a small package. Cash or information, both transferable currencies. Which was it?

I toyed with the idea of calling out, but it wasn't that far, and anyway the exercise would do me good. If I crept up on him unannounced, I might even discover what he was up to. So, I started to walk.

I had only taken a dozen or so steps when my mistake became clear. Within those few seconds, the hard-hearted frost clawed at my head, hands and face. God, it was cold. *Go back and get your coat*, I told myself. But stubborn man that I am, I wouldn't allow myself to be defeated by a such a short journey and I carried on.

It was then that the bloated clouds, hanging so low that I might have reached out and pulled them into my arms, intervened. The first lazy soot-grey flakes rapidly became heavier and thicker until I could see little beyond the end of my nose. I kept moving.

"It's far too cold to snow," I told myself, shivering uncontrollably and recalling my mother's wisdom on the subject. *Too cold to snow in Southern England it might be, but not here*, I reminded myself.

Every breath now became a powdered-glass nightmare, rasping through my mouth, burning up my nose and scorching down my throat until the flakes settled as a freezing slab at the base of my lungs. Soon, I could no longer feel my feet. It seemed they had detached themselves from my legs and journeyed somewhere on their own.

I began to worry. Had I chosen an expedition too far? I imagined the headlines in *Pravda*: 'English Spy Freezes in Dash to Car.' How embarrassing.

Things, of course, could only get worse and did. As my hair retreated from my ears, becoming little more than a tangled knot at the top of my head, it pulled my face so tight that I was afraid the skin might tear. Alarmed, I began to run but my legs joined my feet in protest and, refusing to follow orders, buckled under me. On hands and knees, I tried to crawl but in which direction? I could no longer see the car.

It was then that I knew that I was going to die.

Without warning and for the briefest of moments, the clouds parted and there, in the pale moonlight, only a foot or two in front of me, was the beige blob of rusted metal that was Andrei Andreyevich's Moskvitch. A poor relation to Dmitry's Volga saloon I had always thought, but now the most welcome of sights. As I stretched my bare hand towards the door, Andrei Andreyevich, with a speed and focus I had never seen in him before or since, knocked it away with a thickly gloved hand. Grabbing the metal handle, he pulled the door open and pushed me inside, face-planting me onto the back seat. Following me in, he leaned forward and, after switching the rather inadequate heater up full, turned to me and screamed: "What stupid f*** thing you playing at? It minus thirty-five."

The drops of his spittle only warm — one would have expected — burnt against my skin, and even had I been able to think clearly, I was too frozen to reply.

Too cold to shiver, an ache radiated from every one of my teeth and my fillings threatened to drop from my head; my fingers and toes throbbed in time to the rapid beat of my heart. Made of ice they might be, but they still delivered a burning torment that spread through my arms and legs before invading the rest of my body. The pain was excruciating and had I been able, I would have screamed. Only a minute ago I had been frightened I would die, now I was terrified that I wouldn't.

Outburst over, Andrei Andreyevich climbed out of the car and, opening the boot, began to rummage through his newly delivered boxes. Through my pain and misery, I imagined I heard the faintest tinkle of rattling glass.

Exploration over, he rejoined me, his expression one of a man who had the remedy for my suffering. That wasn't quite true; his face was more that of someone with the answer to every one of the world's troubles. Opening a grubby label-less bottle, and taking a respectable swig himself, he passed it over, demanding, "Drink. Vodka. The best."

Taking it, I swallowed hard, gasping as the oily spirit burnt its way down my throat, but as it did, my body began to thaw. Then the thought came to me: *I must thank Andrei Andreyevich for saving my life.* Doing my best to speak through my pain, and my now numbed tongue, I stuttered, "Vodka, Dynamo, Yashin. The best."

And as Andrei Andreyevich's face lit up, he gave me a smile so broad that I could see every one of his gold-toothed investments.

A GLANCE THROUGH THE WINDOW

A glance through the window was all it took. An adrenaline rush and an itch in my palms told me everything I needed to know. My burning face and sweat-soaked brow would give the same message to any interested passer-by, I was sure. Never had I desired anything as much as her. In that instant, I knew she had to be mine, but in the same moment I became hers.

Motionless on the other side of the glass, she remained distant from the room's other, merely beautiful, occupants. Her slender neck joining smoothly with her naked mahogany back, tapering to the slimmest of waists was beyond comparison. She was perfect.

Was she available? *She must be*, I told myself. It was that sort of place. But what sort of person would abandon such beauty in this tawdry backstreet den, lost amongst its bigger, red-lit neighbours.

Then, as always, doubt set in. *Dare I?* I asked myself.

Don't even consider it, preached the angel on my right shoulder. *She is out of your league. It would be pointless to even try.*

Maybe, just maybe, you might, his demon companion on the other countered. And with that, joy flooded my soul. A feeling completely new to me.

Having no experience of the etiquette of such establishments, I briefly hesitated before, disregarding all good sense, I opened the door and walked in.

In the gloom, the sallow-faced proprietor's bloodshot eyes regarded me through a greying, greasy fringe that hadn't benefitted from shampoo in weeks. He seemed suspicious. Was there something illicit about her? And, dressed in suit and tie, was I different enough from his regular clientele to make him wonder whether I was laying a trap? I neither knew nor cared.

Holding his gaze, I nodded in her direction and asked the price.

He paused and then, opening a mouth filled with a graveyard of mossy, broken teeth, his forty-a-day voice wheezed, "Four grand and you can take her now."

Four thousand. Every last penny I possessed and some. Could such beauty really be worth that? Perhaps she was unaffordable after all.

Don't delay, whispered my demon, eager to cement his triumph. *Supposing someone else takes her while you stand by indecisive.* I knew he was talking sense, but, even so, I had to be sure.

"Just one touch?" I asked, my embarrassed voice petering away into nothing.

"If you must," the man snorted derisively, "but briefly, and then you pay."

That one moment told me all I needed to know. Handing over my card, I emptied my account and then, with shaking hands, my wallet. Sacrificing everything seemed a small price to pay.

Terrified that even now she might escape, I wasted no time in sitting beside her and, bringing her to me, I caressed that oh-so-perfect neck. Whispering sweet nothings, I traced my fingers down her flawless back and, allowing my arm to encircle her waist, I pulled her tight. Then, strumming her six strings, I was lost in the sound of her perfection.

FAMILY SECRETS

LONDON, JUNE 2010

I watched as Sarah, arms wrapped tightly around herself, stared at the near-seventy-year-old painting. She had been standing in the back of my cramped London gallery for five minutes now and, as far as I could tell, in all that time had not taken a single breath. I was becoming increasingly concerned for her welfare. The last thing I needed was for our first contact in over a year to end in a siren-filled dash to the local A & E. In the end, it was my nerve that broke first.

"Tell me," I said, "the woman in the picture, it's David's Uncle Tom, isn't it?"

She sucked in some air.

Wanting to make sure that now she was finally breathing again, she kept going, and desperate to fill the silence, I carried on. "And to all intents and purposes, he is a she. Or at least dressed that way."

There was a pause. "It's complicated," she answered.

"I expect it is, or was, especially in the 1940s. And you knew about this?"

She shook her head, following it with a nod. "Not at first, no, but more recently, yes."

"Are you going to explain?"

"I'll try."

"I think you should. But first, if you don't mind me asking, where the hell have you been?"

Her eyes filled with tears. "Don't."

I felt a pang of guilt. She was obviously struggling, but I had every right to know. Fourteen months – every day wondering whether she was still alive and, if she was, why she had left – had taken their toll on me. The silence continued until my frustration and rage finally boiled over.

"On the day of David's funeral of all days, how could you? You couldn't even be bothered to hang around long enough to say goodbye. And after all he had done for you." I wasn't sure whether my anger was on David's behalf or mine. Actually, it didn't matter. What was important was that I was right.

"Please don't shout," she sobbed. "Don't you think that it haunts me every day."

The rage leaked out of me. Reaching out, intending to pat her shoulder, to show that I understood or was at least sympathetic to her situation, I half expected her to pull away. Instead, she buried her face, complete with streaming make-up, into my chest; my newish white shirt would be ruined forever. I pulled her to me and, kissing the top of her head, told her that everything would be okay, although I had no real idea what the problem was or what form 'okay' would take. Eventually her tears subsided.

"Let's get a cup of tea," I said. "Then you can tell me all about it." At that moment, what I was about to hear didn't really matter.

"I've got a better idea…" she whispered.

*

It was a few months after Sarah's disappearance that I first came across the painting. Quite by chance I was taking a half-hearted wander through the minor lots of a mediocre auction, somewhere in Kent, when I was distracted by a portrait of a young woman. Little more than a foot high, it showed her, hands clasped on lap, sitting ramrod straight on a high-backed chair. Dressed in a cream silk dress that ended just below her knees and accompanied by a fox fur stole that obscured her bare shoulders, her hair was extravagantly styled in, what I believe they called, a permanent wave. Exuding wealth and privilege, she appeared to be everything one might expect of a young lady of means about to embark on her journey into society.

Staring straight back at the artist, she exhibited that same overwhelming disappointment in life I remembered so well. It was this that gave her away. Uncle Tom might have been bent and leather-skinned from a life working the land when I knew him, but those violet eyes transfixing even into his eighties were unmistakable. Although, neither Tom nor this woman, I remembered, were the only persons who possessed such a gaze.

Extracting my loupe from the pocket of the Liberty's waistcoat I always wore to such events, I tried to find an artist's signature. I was disappointed. The painting was so deeply ingrained in grime and grease that I couldn't find one, even had it existed. The sale catalogue was a little more forthcoming, however: The Hon. Thomasina Sanderson on the eve of her wedding, October 1941.

In one of his more lucid moments, David had told me that his Uncle Tom had been married about a year before he was born, so the timing worked. Uncle Tom, the perfect bride-to-be.

I toyed with the idea of bidding, but this was not a work I could easily move. Even had David been alive, his mind by the time I met him was too far gone to allow me to explain where the painting had come from. Anyway, money was, as always, tight and an altruistic purchase such as this would not only be wasted but would likely tip me into bankruptcy. With a shrug, I moved on to other, hopefully more promising, pastures.

*

"Lot seventeen. Full-length painting of a young lady. Artist unknown. Dated 1941. From a label on the back, however, we can be fairly sure that the subject is The Hon. Thomasina Sanderson. Who will offer me one thousand pounds?"

There followed a silence so profound that even the auctioneer seemed uncomfortable. Clearing his throat, he continued. "Five hundred pounds. Will anyone bid me five hundred?" This time his announcement was met with not only silence, but an uncomfortable shuffling of feet. Still there was no bid.

Embarrassed on behalf of my now-departed acquaintance and his family, I raised my hand. "250." I paused and then added, "Guineas."

For some reason, this small addition made the bid seem so much more acceptable.

"I am bid 250 guineas. Do I hear three hundred?" The silence was oppressive. "Pounds?" he added as an afterthought. Quickly calculating that no further bids were forthcoming and perhaps wanting to make sure I didn't have time to regret my offer, he crashed his gavel to the desk. "Sold to the man in the colourful waistcoat at 250 guineas."

And that was how Uncle Tom became part of my collection. Not knowing what else to do with her, I hung the painting in the darkest recess of the gallery and that was where she stayed, unnoticed and forgotten until the morning Sarah walked back into my life.

*

My gallery, in an unfashionable district of South-East London, does not suffer much from passing trade. I make most of my money from hiring out the space for corporate product launches and executive anniversaries or retirements. Once the warm Aldi Chardonnay has flowed semi-freely, someone with more money than sense will occasionally make me an offer, which, if I am lucky, will generate sufficient profit to allow me to eat.

That was why I was somewhat surprised when early one Saturday, the jangling of the bell attached to the front door told me that someone had wandered in from the high street. Fully expecting my visitor to be seeking directions to the local fried chicken shop or desperate for a borrow of the toilet, I didn't hurry.

I am not a cruel man and as long as my visitors feign at least a little interest in my collection, I normally show them some mercy and allow them to use the loo. I couldn't blame them for not wanting to use the public lavs opposite. Flooded and smelling of little more than impatience, a visit there certainly requires a stronger stomach than I possess.

Today, I was wrong. Standing there, as though she had just popped out for a flat white ten minutes earlier, was Sarah my fiancée, or should I say ex-fiancée. I had heard nothing from her since the night before David's funeral. No calls, no postcards, nothing.

I struggled for a smart remark but, in the end, all I managed was, "Hello, Sarah."

"Is that it? After all this time. No 'where have you been?' No 'get out of here, you bitch, you broke my heart.' Just 'hello!'"

Not rising to the bait, I replied, "I've had that conversation in my head so many times, it seems a little pointless now you have finally shown up."

She deflated a little and shuffled her feet. Uncertainty wasn't something I normally associated with her, and I felt a little sad on her behalf.

"I am glad to see you though. I have something I want to show you."

She rolled her eyes heavenwards.

"No, not that. A painting."

"Oh, okay." She seemed a little disappointed.

"I think. No, I don't think, I'm pretty sure that it's of David's Uncle Tom."

"You are joking."

I shook my head, and after turning the door sign from open to closed, I took her arm and led her to the back of the gallery. At one point she leant into me. I liked that feeling.

For some reason, I had bought a rather fetching stainless-steel lamp to place above the painting in case anyone wanted a better view. Unlikely, I knew, but you never could tell. Switching it on, I stood back and watched as Sarah got her first sight of Uncle Tom at his womanly best and failed to breathe.

*

I first met Sarah in 2005, when she ran into the shop one rainy and windswept Saturday afternoon, chasing after a rather overexcited David. As they had passed by, David had become smitten by a painting in the window and rushed inside. Before either of us had any chance to stop him, he had climbed into the window space and was caressing the canvas with the ends of his oh-so-long fingers.

"I'm so sorry," she said in that breathless way of hers, "we'll pay you for any damage done."

"I wouldn't worry, I'm sure that anything he does can only be an improvement," I replied. "To be honest, it is only there to discourage true art lovers from entering. However," I added "if he starts to lick it, I may be forced to change my mind."

"It might be that we have to buy it anyway if I want to get him out of here." She glanced at the price tag. "I'm sure we can manage that, as long as you give us a reasonable discount."

While we left David free to explore the rest of the collection, Sarah and I sat in the back room drinking tea from stained and chipped mugs while she dunked digestives – her favourites, I discovered. She had, she told me, been David's carer for just over two years. She had been offered the job on the day of her graduation. Panic rising at the realisation that she would now have to pay back her debts and that there was no way she could ever earn enough to achieve that, she was surprised when an elderly stranger, Uncle Tom as it turned out, approached and offered her a job. The pay was good; actually, it was unbelievable, and the work was easy. All that was expected of her was to tidy up and ensure that David didn't wander out into the traffic. In those days, David was still pretty much aware of his surroundings; the micro-strokes he suffered many times each day had not yet stolen all his memories. It was an offer she couldn't refuse, especially as it gave her time to pursue her further studies. An endeavour encouraged by both Uncle Tom and David.

"What are you studying?" I asked.

"A PhD in the history of art," she replied.

Oh dear, I thought. "Didn't you question the offer?" I asked.

"No, not really," she told me. "I was so desperate I would have done anything."

"Surely not anything," I queried.

"Anything!" she replied and touched my hand.

Somewhere later in the conversation, she let slip that Sundays were her day off; she liked visiting galleries; she had tickets for an exhibition the next weekend and had no one to go with. I took the hint.

And the rest, as they say, is history.

*

"I've got a better idea…"

It was dark when I awoke, shivering. That shouldn't have come as a surprise; I was lying in bed naked and sans duvet. I was also alone. As I lay there wondering whether Sarah had disappeared yet again, I was reassured by the sound of a kettle boiling in the distance. Unless I had a very considerate burglar, it seemed that she was in the kitchen making tea.

My suspicions were soon confirmed as I heard her struggling up the very steep stairs. I was tempted to go and help but decided that some punishment was due for the quilt theft and so I left her to it.

Pushing the door open with her bottom, Sarah backed into the room. She had wrapped herself in the quilt, which she was holding in place with her arms while at the same time carrying a tray. I had a tray? On it, she had placed two steaming mugs of what smelled like tea, a half-empty packet of chocolate digestives and a small leather-bound notebook. I was intrigued.

She deposited the tea on the bedside tables and, pointing to the biscuits with her eyes, said, "I thought we might need something to keep us going. We may be a long time."

I raised my eyebrows. "I'm not sure I am up to that just at the moment."

"Do you never think of anything else?" She smiled. "It was rather nice though."

"I'm surprised I managed to perform at all. It has been over a year."

"You waited. That's good to know."

Getting back into bed, she returned a small fraction of the duvet and, after taking a swig of tea, leaned against the bedhead. Pulling her knees up to her chest, she began her tale.

"Before I start," she told me, "you need to understand that I only found out about the book," she waved it at me, "the night before David's funeral. Reading it, I went a little crazy."

"A whole year crazy?"

"Pretty much. Even so, what's in the book isn't the most surprising thing I discovered."

"What else?"

"Later."

Settling herself down, she began Uncle Tom's story. She didn't need the notebook at all; it was apparent that every detail was safely locked in her memory. However, she did occasionally refer to it as she went along. Mainly dates, I think.

This is how it went.

Uncle Tom was indeed a woman marrying David's father in 1941. The back of the painting must have been referring to this marriage. It appears that it was not a happy union and, shortly after David was born, the pair split. David stayed with his father, while Thomasina went to live in London, where it seems that she took up with a rather shady character she referred to as the Colonel.

"At first, I thought the Colonel might be Thomasina's father," Sarah told me. "Then I became convinced that he was her lover from long before David's father was on the scene. There are a few hints that she might have known him before she met David's father and even that David might not have been her husband's child, if you know what I mean."

"Was David aware of all this?" I asked.

"If he was, it seems he was remarkably uninterested."

"Are you sure the Colonel wasn't both?" I asked.

"Please!" she replied, wrinkling her nose in disgust. "What a mind you have." Relaxing a bit, she said, "In the end, I decided that, in the beginning at least, he was neither. Just a rather questionable man who seemed to have some sort of insalubrious influence over her."

It appears that, at this time, the Colonel was somehow associated with the government and was looking for people who spoke French. The idea was to land them undercover in France. Thomasina even suspected that this might have been the only reason the Colonel took an interest in her.

"Tom." I couldn't get my mind away from the Tom I had once known. "He spoke French?"

"Fluently. His mother was French, I'm told." She shrugged. "She, he. I can never figure which way to go. Apparently, the military needed someone to lead sabotage work in Marseilles to distract the Germans and their sympathisers. Because the work was in the docks, they wanted a man. You know what people were like in those days. If it was dangerous, a woman was fine. If it was important, they weren't good enough."

"What happened next?"

"It seems that Thomasina and the Colonel simply changed the paperwork and bought a man's suit."

"So, Thomasina became Tom."

"Apparently so. She must have been good at it, as it appears that other than a brief period in the fifties, she pretty much stayed that way for the rest of her life."

"I never suspected a thing," I told her. "She must have gained some weight after having David. The Tom in the painting could never have got away with it."

According to Sarah, what happened next was rather sketchy in Tom's notes, but it appearred that the disguised fishing boat being used to transport Tom to the South of France was torpedoed in the Mediterranean and went down with all hands.

"Not all hands."

"Obviously not."

Some days later, Tom was washed ashore, battered and unconscious, his lungs full of water. He was discovered by French partisans who nursed him back to health. Whether they ever checked on his real nature or weren't bothered when they found out is unclear, but once he recovered, Tom joined them and became a full member of their group. As he already had French paperwork and spoke native French, it seems that deceiving the authorities was a reasonably easy matter.

Once the war was over, and as he had no real reason to go back to England, Tom remained with his rescuers working the land. He fitted in so well that no one questioned his presence until one day when, for some reason, he decided to visit Paris. On his first evening there, he got roaring drunk and into a fight with a Gendarme, ending up in a cell. Even then, he might have got away with it had the police not decided to give him a shower before he appeared in front of the magistrate. At this point, Tom's secret was, as you might imagine, well and truly revealed and his masquerade uncovered.

Of course, when approached, the British Government denied all knowledge of him. Having a spy working undercover to discover the hidden secrets of the French rural economy was not something they wanted to own up to. They were not believed, of course, although in this case they were absolutely right. Tom was sentenced to five years for espionage. However, after a secret intervention – Tom thought from the Colonel via his old war channels – his sentence was commuted, and he was simply deported back to the UK.

Tom arrived in England late in 1951, only to discover that he had been declared missing and presumed dead. After a short debriefing, and as the security services wanted nothing at all to do with him, he was given a train ticket back to his last registered address and sent packing. Now back as Thomasina, she arrived home on Christmas Eve to find that her husband, thinking her dead, had remarried less than forty-eight hours after her death certificate had been issued.

"How did Tom feel about that?"

"He doesn't say. He only mentions feeling a bit miffed that by this time David was referring to the new wife as Ma. It must have been a bit of a shock though. What really pissed him off was that never having officially landed in France, he received no recognition for his service. He was very bitter about this. In particular, he blamed the Colonel for betraying him. Although, as you will see, Tom seems to have forgiven him pretty quickly."

While Thomasina might have quite rightly made a fuss about the situation, thus bringing shame and embarrassment on the whole family, instead she quietly made her way to London, cocooned herself in a backstreet hotel in Pimlico and, after a few days, which she seems to have spent in quiet enjoyment with the now-forgiven Colonel, she re-emerged as a bright new man about town. In this guise, she returned to her family as Uncle Tom, pretty much remaining so for the rest of her days.

"And now," Sarah told me. "It really starts to get weird. While New Wife remained steadfastly barren, it was not long before Tom was thickening around the waist."

"What happened next?"

"It's a bit complicated. Like some cheap Victorian novel, Tom was sent back to Pimlico with the Colonel, only returning as Uncle Tom, once again, a few months later when his middle had returned to normal."

After Tom returned from Pimlico, the sleeping arrangements seemed to have carried on much as they had before. However, with New Wife unable to reproduce and Tom being more careful, there were no further alarms and, to all intents and purposes, David remained an only, if rather delicate, child. This state of affairs might have carried on forever were it not for the fact that one night David's father, after the apparent excesses of engaging in a threesome, had a fatal heart attack. According to the notebook, some shuffling around occurred before the authorities were called. It seems that no one suspected anything untoward and not long after the funeral, Tom, now being the *man* of the house, simply switched rooms, becoming a permanent occupant of New Wife's bed. Everything then carried on much as before until a couple of years later when New Wife also passed on. At this point, Tom seems to have decided that he was far too old to make yet another change and dedicated the rest of his life to looking after David as a father rather than a mother.

"And David never knew?"

"I don't think he did."

"Curiouser and curiouser. This is beginning to sound like an episode from *Eastenders*."

Sarah gave me her special hard stare, one that would have put Paddington to shame. "It's late; let's finish this tomorrow."

"But what happened to the child?"

"I said tomorrow." She shivered and, putting down the book, snuggled up. "Hold me," she ordered.

I did as I was told, marvelling at the softness of her skin.

*

It was the next evening before we continued Uncle Tom's tale. All day, Sarah had avoided the subject and carried on as though there was nothing hanging in the air between us. By mid-afternoon, I had concluded that there must be little more to tell. How wrong I was.

As it got dark, she pushed herself as far into the corner of the settee as she could, making herself as small as possible.

"The evening before David's funeral," she began. "His solicitor called me and told me about Tom's other child, a girl."

"What had happened to her?"

"All he knew was that she had been given up for adoption to a childless couple who were paid off by the Colonel. Tom never saw her again."

"What did Tom know of the arrangements?"

"I don't believe he knew much at all. If he ever asked, I think the Colonel told him that everything was going well, and it was best to let sleeping dogs lie. Actually, I don't think the Colonel had any contact either. To all intents and purposes, she ceased to exist."

What the solicitor did know was that, a few years previously, the Colonel had also passed, leaving his considerable estate in trust to the daughter with instructions for Tom to find her. Unfortunately, by this time it appears that Tom was far more focused on finding a suitable carer for his here-and-now son, rather than the long-lost daughter he had only known for a few hours.

"At the time, I didn't know why he chose me, and why he turned up at my graduation, but I am grateful that he did. As you know, I have no parents. It was wonderful to have someone to watch me graduate, even a complete stranger. Tom offered me the job then and there. Then, when he passed, the arrangement with David stayed pretty much the same."

"But what about when David died?"

"That was when everything changed. The solicitor called me and asked whether I had anywhere to go. When I said no, he gave me the notebook and told me I could stay living in the house being paid the same salary until I found the daughter. By now, not only would she inherit the Colonel's estate, but also that of Tom and David. I believe he thought he was doing me a favour, although within hours I began to have my doubts."

For a moment, I wondered whether Sarah might be the long-lost daughter, but the timing was out, by a couple of decades at least.

"So, you spent the night before David's funeral reading Tom's book and decided to do a runner."

"Pretty much, yes. I'm not sure why, but I couldn't stay in that place with all its ghosts until I had the answer. I told the solicitor that I would search for the daughter but do it for free and in my own way. It never occurred to me that it would take this long."

"I appreciate that but I'm sad that you didn't feel you could trust me."

"I'm sorry. I wanted to, I really did, but the longer I was away, the harder it was to come home."

I thought I knew what was coming but decided to let Sarah tell me in her own time. "What happened next?"

"I went looking for Tom's daughter."

"And?"

"By the time I tracked her down, she was long dead. Apparently, she had struggled with mental health issues all her life. I think these days you would call her bipolar. Anyway, as a teenager, she ran away from her adoptive family and went to live in London. By this point, she was a heavy drug user and working the streets. It seems she carried on this way for over ten years until, in 1982, she was found dead in a public toilet in Leicester Square – an overdose."

"And Tom did nothing about this?"

"I'm sure he didn't know, or of course he would have intervened. I found out one more thing. The year before she died, the daughter had a child, also a girl. She was taken into care for her own welfare."

"You were born in 1981," I whispered, but if she heard me, she ignored it. "And all this took you over a year?"

"No, I found out about Tom's daughter quite quickly, but I needed to find out something more and that is what took the time."

"What more did you need?"

"The final piece of the puzzle. The identity and whereabouts of his granddaughter." She pulled out some papers. "Birth certificates, adoption papers, the missing link to the inheritance. I finally sorted it two days ago and then I came home."

That was twice she had mentioned home. And where is home, I wanted to ask but I was too afraid of what the answer might be. So, instead, I asked, "Who is she, this granddaughter?"

She stared at me hard, those wonderful violet eyes, identical to those of David and Uncle Tom, looking back at me, just like in the portrait.

"Me, you muppet. Haven't you figured it out yet? You are slow."

I could have said something, but why spoil her big reveal?

"The Colonel may have been my grandfather, who knows." She continued, "Uncle Tom was definitely my grandmother and David, my uncle. As their only living relative, I inherit everything."

Of course, I had realised this hours ago, about the time she reminded me that Tom had hunted her down and offered her the job, but she needed to tell the story in her own way. So, I had kept my mouth shut.

"Everything? House, land, everything?" I asked.

She nodded. "Everything. It seems that I am a very wealthy woman indeed."

An earlier thought pushed its way back into my head. Home.

"You said earlier, you had come home. Tell me, where is home?"

"Here, with you. If you'll have me back."

"Have I told you that now you are extremely rich, you have suddenly become very attractive to me?"

She smiled and, leaning over, kissed me hard, pushing the tip of her tongue against my teeth.

"I'm so glad you feel that way and, unless you have other ideas, I think it's time for bed."

THE DEEP DARK WOODS

"Does it get any easier?" Bob, my newly appointed DC asked. Green behind the ears, he might have been at the start of his first shift out of uniform, but not as grassy as his face was now.

"No, I'm afraid it doesn't. If it's a child, it's even worse," I replied. "So be grateful for what we have."

Bob looked away. Was he going to throw up? Never a good sign on your first day. But Bob was made of stern stuff and instead he took a deep breath and, turning back to the corpse lying in its shallow grave, asked, "What do we do next?"

Without replying, I pulled my latex gloves over my sausage-like fingers and knelt down slowly and carefully. When you are my size, slow and careful is the only way you move, especially when there is mud.

"Talk to me," I said.

"Dog walker called it in about an hour ago. The rain had washed some of the earth away. That was how he saw her. The dog helped a little," he added, glancing at his notes. "Then uniform arrived and uncovered her completely."

"Why?"

"They thought there was a chance she was still alive."

I glanced at the body and then at him. "Seems unlikely."

"I know, but it was still half dark at the time. They probably couldn't see the state she was in."

"When did you get here?"

"About ten minutes ago. First thing I did was secure the scene."

Looking at the many footprints around the makeshift grave, his actions had been far too late, but well done him for thinking it through. Pulling a lock of congealed hair, darker than I remembered, away from her spoiled head, I feigned surprise. It had been over fifteen years since we were at school, but I had never doubted for one moment that this was what life had in store for her.

Struggling to stand, I slipped in the morass that was now the surrounding area and half fell across her body. Had it not been for Bob's strong arm, I would have crushed her completely.

"Thanks. Sorry about that. I better call it in."

The Head of Serious Crimes (HSC) answered on the second ring. "Hi, it's Andy. Victim: blonde woman, aged thirty-three, looks to have been deceased only a few hours. Battered to death, by the looks of it. But we have a problem; rather, two problems."

I heard her sigh. "What is it?"

"Well, for one, I know her. Name is Hyacinth Pendleton, and two, I have compromised the scene."

The silence at the other end lasted an eternity. "How?" she asked eventually.

"It's very muddy up here; slipped and fell."

"We've no one to replace you. Talk to the Scene of Crime Officers (SOCO) when they get there and get a swab done. We will have to do the best we can."

That was good, SOCO would now cover me for any mistakes I might have made.

"An ex of yours?" asked Bob as I hung up.

"Hardly. Knew her at school. Right bitch." I was surprised at the venom with which that came out, but not as surprised as Bob, who took an actual step back, eyes widening.

"Sorry," I said, "uncalled for." But it wasn't, it was totally deserved. I had never recovered from the only time she had acknowledged me. I meant every word of it.

She had been standing in the school corridor surrounded by her acolytes. With her skirt rolled up at the waist to reveal as much of her shapely legs as possible, her oversized glasses deliberately chosen no doubt to give her a look of intelligence, she was probably the most beautiful creature I had ever seen. The worst thing was that she was the smartest kid in the class and knew it, and I was the slowest. She knew that as well.

As I lumbered past, doing my best to make myself invisible, not invisible enough as it turned out, one of her group took a sudden step back, spearing her high heel deep into my foot. Heels were strictly against school rules obviously, but no one would dare challenge Hyacinth or any of her crew. I think I screamed out loud.

Hyacinth turned to me and sneered. "Watch out, Porky. There isn't room for anyone else when you are in the corridor." The others laughed and pointed.

That cannot be true, I thought. Pleasantly plump

perhaps, big boned maybe, but fat? Never. But the truth, buried deep, rushed to the surface and, burning red, I died inside.

Bob cleared his throat, bringing me back to the miserable surroundings and the task in hand.

"Sorry," I said. "I was miles away, remembering her from school. Trying to think of anything that might be relevant."

"And was there?"

"No," I lied.

By this time, SOCO had arrived. Taping off the scene, they erected a plastic tent over the grave and were now laying out a series of numbered plastic markers and taking pictures. Until they had completed their preliminary examination, there was little more we could do.

"Drive us into the village and let's get some breakfast," I said. "I'm starving."

Bob didn't need any persuasion and fifteen minutes later, we were seated in the local cozy café, warming our hands around mugs of steaming builders' tea.

"Not much use us doing a house-to-house around here. It's fairly isolated, so no one will have seen anything," I spluttered, splattering Bob with crumbs from my second bacon butty. With only the slightest of winces, he brushed himself clean.

"The bad news," I told him, "is that I need you to go back and chat to dog walkers, hikers, and the like. You will need to stay there until after work."

He looked at me quizzically.

"That's when the couples turn up," I continued. "I want you to talk to them, 'specially the ones that are married, but not to each other."

"Why them?"

"They always worry about getting caught," I explained. "So, they notice everything that goes on. It's gonna be a long day for you," I added.

Bob's shoulders slumped.

"Got a heavy date then?"

"No, sir."

"Good. That means you can stay even later and question the doggers as well."

Bob raised his eyes heavenward, perhaps uttering a silent prayer. I did my best to feel some sympathy for him but failed.

By the time we got back, SOCO was preparing to move the body. It would go to the mortuary and, as it was a suspicious death, a full autopsy would be carried out to establish a cause. Not that there was any doubt in my mind.

I walked over to their van.

"Any ideas?" I slurred as they poked a swap under my tongue and along the inside of my cheek, moving it around as if they were trying to hoover up all the leftover bits of bacon.

"Multiple blows with something cylindrical. The skull is crushed, and the brains have leaked, but that wasn't what actually killed her."

"What did?"

"I'll get to that in a minute. Whoever did this took a real dislike to her."

Not the only one, I thought as I watched Bob turn pale yet again. *Has his bacon-and-egg roll disagreed with him?* I wondered.

"There are traces of wood and paint in the wounds," SOCO continued, "so should be easy enough to identify the weapon."

"Golf club?" I asked.

"No, something bigger."

"Baseball bat?"

SOCO looked at me strangely. "Yes, that would work. Why do you say that?"

"Got one at home to frighten intruders," I replied. "Anything else?"

"No sign of sexual activity in the hours either side of death." He paused. "Also, she might have died here but the attack took place somewhere else. Not enough blood at the scene. She mostly bled out there."

"What does that mean?"

"She was alive when she was buried. She suffocated."

That was enough for Bob who, despite doing his best to get to the trees in time, compromised the scene even further.

As it would be a while before SOCO had anything useful to add, I went back to the station and started the process of gathering data on the victim and potential suspects. About four, I phoned Bob for an update. Cold, hungry and wet, he had so far learnt little of any use. While the dog walkers had on the whole been helpful, they had seen nothing. No doubt he would discover some much more interesting titbits once it got dark; I hoped he was broad-minded.

With nothing else to do at the station, I headed back to the wood, but changing my mind drove home instead. Shattered from lack of sleep, I quickly dropped off in my armchair. Within seconds, I was dreaming about last night.

*

Thud, my body juddered as I drove the spade into the rich, dark earth. I had been digging for over an hour. If I didn't get a move on, it would be light before I finished. Despite my aches, an ever-growing exhaustion and the sweat pouring like a small stream from every pore, I kept going. Thud, judder. Thud, judder. Would I ever finish?

The anger that drove me had absorbed my days and dreams for the last fifteen years, never fading but always festering deep inside me. For all that time, rage had been my unremitting companion. Then, Lady Luck had smiled on me, and I had finally been given my chance. In none of my fantasies had I imagined her delivering herself by turning up unannounced on my doorstep. Nevertheless, it would have been ungrateful not to have seized the opportunity once it arrived, so of course I took it. Porky indeed.

I had recognised her the minute I answered the door. Did I show any surprise? If I had, she failed to notice. My first thoughts were that the bitch had finally come to beg my forgiveness, but I quickly realised that she had no idea who I was. To her, I was a complete stranger, a nonentity, and even had she remembered me, she would probably have been unable to recall my name. And why should she? Stuck out here in my small house hidden in the woods, I had put on at least one hundred pounds since she had last seen me. Occasionally, however, size can be turned to your advantage. It makes you all but invisible to women.

"Can you help me?" she asked, and like it was yesterday I shuddered as her high-pitched nasal whine brought back every nuance of my humiliation. She was the reason I had never married, had a girlfriend, had any social life to speak of, or friends outside of work. I was pretty much a total recluse.

"My car has run out of petrol and my mobile isn't working," she continued.

"There isn't a proper signal around here," I responded, "and no one much other than me until you get into town."

I allowed the enormity of what I was saying sink in and watched as she shrank in front of me. If I didn't help, she would have a five-mile walk to the nearest phone box.

"I am afraid I don't have any spare fuel," I lied, "but I can give you a ride into town."

From the curl of her lip and the narrowing of her eyes, I could tell that she looked upon that prospect with distaste. She had not changed at all. Mind you, I could understand why she wouldn't want to be with me; I didn't much like spending time with me either.

"You can use my landline to call the AA," I added.

She hesitated, not out of recognition but because both options would involve her being alone with me and that made her uncomfortable.

It was then I turned on the charm. "I have one of those wireless phone thingies," I said, smiling. "Let me get it for you and you can phone from out here." With any luck, that offer would put her at her ease.

I was right, and as she relaxed, she gave me a brief smile.

"Thanks."

Indoors, my mind raced. All that time had passed, yet the pain was still there, like it was only yesterday. "One day," I had stuttered in reply to the Porky comment, "you will beg to go out with me."

"Go out with you?" she replied. "I would rather die!"

And now she would.

Doing my best to keep my breathing even, I gathered up my phone, a copy of the Yellow Pages and, most important of all, my baseball bat. I did think of getting my shotgun from the cupboard, but that would have been too obvious, and besides, it would be much too quick and painless. After nearly half a lifetime spent in torment, I owed her something far worse.

Quietly placing the bat just inside the front door, I went outside and handed her the directory and phone. She smiled gratefully and walked away a few paces. I knew that this would happen. It is what people do when they are having a telephone conversation with a stranger present, and so I was ready to act as soon as her back was turned.

Picking up the bat, I headed towards her as silently as I could manage. Not quietly enough it turned out, because as I held the bat high above her head, she must have caught a slight stirring in the air. Turning to face me, her eyes widening in horror, she emitted a silent scream and backed away, but she was too late. As I crashed the bat down as hard as my strength would allow, I was comforted by the sound of splintering bones as it embedded itself into her face and head.

Crumpling to the ground, she twitched violently. Only then did the blood flow. I had expected it to spurt, but instead a slow, glutinous mix of blood and brain matter oozed from her crushed eye socket, staining the dirt around my feet in an ever-expanding arc of liquid darkness. She moaned and it was then that my years of frustration exploded, and I was hitting her again and again, not stopping until the bat split along its length.

As I stood over her, struggling for breath, an element of sanity returned and my training kicked in. I couldn't leave her here; eventually someone would report her missing and a search would quickly find her car close to my driveway. I had to move them both.

Taking a can from my shed, I walked down to the road and poured enough petrol into the tank to take us a few miles. Squeezing myself into the driver's seat of her tiny but exorbitantly expensive car, I used the keys she had conveniently left in the ignition to start the engine.

Packing a body into a boot is, I discovered, surprisingly difficult, even when the loader is a big as me and the loaded as small as her. Not that I could have known; it wasn't anything I had attempted before or, on reflection, planned to try again. Anyway, ten minutes later, hot and pouring sweat, I had got her inside. In another five, after squashing some of her extremities, I managed to close the lid.

There is a small clearing in the woods on the other side of the hill from my place. Parking up as far into the trees as I could manage, I abandoned the car and used the nearby logging track to stroll home. I didn't need to go anywhere near the road. In the distance, a church clock struck midnight.

Back home, I poured myself a large whisky into the only uncracked tumbler I possessed and sat down in front of the TV. But try as I might, I couldn't unwind. The memory of her bloodied body lying near my front door came back time and again and I began to worry whether I had made some mistakes.

Of course I had. Someone was sure to find the car and call it in. Then when the local plods got around to responding, they would discover Hyacinth and the proverbial would hit the fan. If they found the car, but not her, they might just assume it had been stolen then abandoned and not think too deeply about it until she was reported missing. To buy myself time, I had to move her away from the car.

Collecting a spade, I used it to cover up the blood stains on my drive as best I could. Then, getting into my Mitsubishi, I used its wide wheels to obliterate the skinny little tyre tracks her Mini had left. Now no one would know that she had ever been near my place. Five minutes later, after parking at the logging trail, I walked through the woods, spade in hand, to a quiet spot I knew and began digging.

*

Thud, judder. Thud, judder. It would soon get light. I couldn't take the risk of being spotted, so I would have to make the best of what I had. Anyway, the hole looked deep enough, and it was far enough away from her car to prevent the body from being found easily.

Wheezing, I stumbled back to where I had parked her car to find nothing. The boot lid was open, but the boot was empty. If my heart had been pounding earlier, it was nothing compared to now as a tightening band of pain wrapped itself around my chest and pushed its way down my left arm. My knees trembled and had I not had a nearby tree to lean against, I am sure that SOCO would have had two bodies to deal with.

My mind raced. What should I do? Had she managed to find her way to the road and flag down a passing car? Or, worse still, had she called for help from her mobile? There was a signal of sorts here. A squad car might already be on its way. Given the state she was in, it was unlikely, but you never knew.

"Shit! This cannot be happening to me. It's so unfair," I screamed to the trees. All I had wanted was for her to go through a tiny portion of the pain I had experienced over the years, and I couldn't even get that right.

Pulling myself together, losing control like that wasn't going to help at all, I noticed a trail of blood leading from the car. I followed it until, some yards away, I found her unconscious but still breathing. Somehow, despite all her injuries, she had managed to scramble out of the boot and away. She was so much stronger than I had given her credit for. The good news was that, almost blind and desperate, she had managed to drag herself away from any chance of safety and was now much closer to her own grave. Excellent, I had been unsure whether I had enough strength left to haul her the whole distance but now she had done most of the work for me.

Bending over and seizing her wrists, I tensed my worn-out muscles and slowly pulled her to the edge of the open pit, then, kicking her hard, I let gravity do the rest. I watched with macabre fascination as she silently slid into her tomb and lay scrunched at the bottom. Then, grabbing my spade, I started piling earth onto her. As the first load fell across her chest, she moaned and, opening her remaining eye, stared at me out of the wreckage of that once-beautiful face. Finally, she recognised me and whimpered.

"Please, perhaps we could go out somewhere and talk about it."

I said nothing. That offer had come far too late.

Looking deep into my eyes, she saw her own answer and as I watched with overwhelming satisfaction, all hope died in her. I resumed shovelling and as the earth covering her deepened, her moans faded until she was silent.

Grave filled and earth tamped down, I finally allowed myself some rest. Squatting down beside a tall fir tree, I struck a match on its rough bark and lit a cigarette. Pulling the acrid smoke deep into my lungs, I looked at my handiwork and took pleasure in it.

Then it began to rain. That was good; it would wash away the blood. But as it turned out, the rain was not good news at all.

Job done, I drove home and got into bed. I was still fast asleep when Bob woke me with the news that someone had found a body.

*

For the second time that day, I woke to a ringing phone. My body stiff and sore from being scrunched up in the chair, I struggled to come to. By now, it was dark.

"Hello."

"It's Bob, sir. I took a wander around the woods as you suggested and found a car hidden amongst the trees.

I checked with DVLA, and it belongs to the victim. SOCO has just got back. I think you should join us."

I imagined the scene, then, shuddering back to reality, realised that Bob was still talking.

"The keys were still in the ignition, sir, so I got them dusted."

Why hadn't I worn gloves? I asked myself. I wouldn't be able to explain that one to SOCO. But my ordeal wasn't over.

"I also checked the satnav history," he told me. "The car seems to have been stopped on a road a little way away for some time before being driven here."

"SOCO must have been right about the body being moved," I interrupted.

"That's what I thought. Do you want me to come over to your place?" he asked. "I could do with getting dry."

I didn't need him here poking around. "No, it's okay," I answered, sighing. "I need to be there. See you in a few minutes."

I needed to distract him; the last thing I wanted was Bob thinking too closely about where the car might have been or, worse still, noticing how near to my place it was.

Locard had been right, Hyacinth would have left something of herself here despite my best efforts; fingerprints on the phone, blood somewhere I hadn't noticed, and I had most definitely left something of me in that car. I didn't want Bob visiting me anytime soon. At least not until I had had the chance to get the bleach out. To keep his mind elsewhere, I asked, "Anything else before I come over?"

"Yes, sir, a bit of a break. I have found a couple who

stopped for a little *how's your father* on their way into work early this morning. They saw something strange."

"What?" I think I shouted.

"A large man leaning against a tree having a smoke."

"Not much to go on, is it?" I said, calming a little.

"No, sir, but we searched where the witnesses said they saw him. It wasn't far from the scene, and guess what?"

"Tell me."

"We found a match and a cigarette end. There will be DNA."

The band encircled my chest again, and this time it squeezed so hard that I struggled to get air into my lungs.

"He also said," Bob continued, "that he saw the man walk into the woods and get into a Shogun parked on one of the logging trails." He paused. "Don't you have one of those, sir?"

"I do indeed, and they are not that common." I gasped, doing my best to sound normal. "Get back to the DVLA and get a list of all the locally owned silver Shoguns. Also, see whether there are any clues on the logging trail."

There was silence at the other end of the line until Bob said, "Yes, sir. Just one thing. I never mentioned it was silver." He hung up.

Damn! Bob might be green, but he wasn't cabbage-coloured. The younger me would already be talking to HSC making plans and if Bob was half the detective I suspected he was, he would be doing the same right now.

I needed to think fast. I didn't have long – an hour maybe. There were only two possibilities open to me. I could wait, pains worsening, band grasping ever tighter, and hope that my heart exploded long before Bob and the team arrived. Or I could go out with a bang. Whichever path I chose, there was little doubt I would be captured soon.

Only the second option held any appeal. My fantasies of revenge had never been limited to just Hyacinth. She might have created the darkness in me, but there were also her friends. They had embraced her cruelty and laughed at my discomfort.

With what little time I had left, I had to make the others pay. It was time that my dreams of revenge ended and became a reality. My only question was: if I took off now, how many of them could I get before Bob caught up with me?

I took the list of addresses – kept in my desk drawer and regularly updated – and collected my shotgun.

THE GIRL ON THE PINK BICYCLE

At ten on the morning of my eighteenth birthday, I found myself standing on the pavement outside the offices of the stranger who claimed to be my solicitor. Until a month previously, I had not even realised that I had such a thing.

Earlier that day, I had been evicted from the children's home where I had lived for the last twelve years. I had little to show for it: a rucksack of clothes, a ten-pound note and a voucher for a single night's accommodation at the local YMCA. That's not being totally honest. I also had an offer of a place at a prestigious university and a letter from said solicitor inviting me to drop in sometime to learn something to my advantage.

Once I had squandered my one night at the YMCA, my plans were rather sketchy. I intended to spend a couple of days near the university getting my bearings and, once that was done, I had a vague idea of finding some sort of a job to tide me over the summer. So, all in all, it seemed that there was little to lose by visiting the man who had sent me the letter.

The door to the solicitor's office, with its coal-black mirror-like paint and massive lion-head knocker, was breathtaking, like nowhere I had ever been before; so much so that I almost walked away. If only I had. Telling myself nothing ventured and all that and remembering the single-word advantage, I grasped the ring running through the lion's open maw and gave it a stern rap.

The grey-haired old lady who opened the door showed no surprise at finding a rather scruffy teenager with no appointment waiting outside. Instead, with a kindly smile, she led me along a corridor to an open office and showed me inside.

Behind an oversized wooden desk in a stuffy and overheated room sat a bald, scrawny-necked man, his head and oversized eyes starting like a tortoise from an old-fashioned starched collar. My solicitor, I assumed. Standing, he leant his stooped frame across the desk and, giving me a graveyard smile, held out a parchment-skinned hand. It was as though he had been sat there waiting for me. Or perhaps he had no other clients. Either way, I was too embarrassed to ask.

"Can I get you tea or something stronger?" he asked, his thin voice as dry and dusty as the office itself.

Used to being ignored by adults at best or more normally treated with distain, I was a little taken aback at being treated as an equal, but wanting to make an impression, I changed the parameters.

"Coffee, please."

After asking the old lady to get me coffee, he didn't feel the need to tell her what he wanted and continued.

"I believed you would visit today, it being your

eighteenth. Any earlier and we could only have discussed matters in theory, so your timing is perfect."

I mumbled an apology for not making an appointment. He dismissed it with a casual wave and proceeded to make small talk along the lines of how unusually warm it was for this time of year as we waited. The coffee, when it arrived, was in the tiniest cup I have ever seen. It was also accompanied by biscuits to match. His, half-filling a cut-glass tumbler, was obviously of the 'something stronger' variety. As I sipped mine, so hot I almost burnt my mouth, he took a long gulp of his, then, clearing his throat, removed his thick rimless spectacles. Without them, his eyes were an almost normal size. Taking a starched white handkerchief from a drawer in his desk and showing no sign of hurry, he half placed each lens into his mouth and breathed on it. He held the handkerchief between thumb and forefinger as he rubbed the lenses clean. Once satisfied, he passed me a small sheaf of papers.

"Your inheritance, young man. Take your time, and then ask me any questions you may have."

I looked at the papers with their long rows of figures. *There must be a mistake; these numbers are enormous*, I thought. As I pretended to study them, he told me about my parents.

"Although they had very little other than the family house and a small portfolio at the time of their death," he explained. "Due to my sound investments, their value has increased somewhat over the years."

I noticed that he had taken personal credit for the investments, but if what was in front of me was correct, that credit was thoroughly deserved.

Finally able to speak, I asked, "Have I missed something? These numbers seem far too big."

He told me that, yes, they were correct, and that I was now a rather rich young man.

Immediately, his manner changed and, in the sort of voice I suspect he normally reserved for the more lawless elements that passed through this room, he advised me not to let my newly acquired means go to my head. If I was careful, he continued, my inheritance should last me well beyond university and give me some resources to make my way in the world. The way he spoke would not have been out of place in some Dicken's novel or other as he, the family guardian, admonished his young charge to follow a life of rectitude and prudence.

"Do you have any idea what you shall do next?" he asked.

Other than a couple of days away and university, nothing, I was about to say. But the moment I opened my mouth, a mischievous and all together more exciting prospect opened up before me. The world was now my oyster, as they say. Perhaps tasting a few bivalve molluscs would be in order.

"Is there any reason why I shouldn't defer university and go travelling?" I asked.

I expected an immediate rebuttal – the standard answer I received at the home to any idea I raised. His answer was a long time coming, but when it came, it surprised me. Other than warning me not to stay in five-star hotels too frequently and some recommendations on which parts of Bangkok to avoid or visit depending on my particular vices, he thought it an excellent suggestion. So, instead of going to university, I went travelling.

The problem with changing plans without thinking them through is that they have unintended consequences. A spur-of-the-moment decision can come back to bite you and that is what happened to me, but it would be four years before I fully understood its significance.

*

Just short of twelve months later – lean, sun-bronzed, brimming with experiences and the proud owner of a new and still rather itchy tattoo – I finally got around to continuing my education. As I still knew very little about the town where I would be studying, I decided that my original idea of spending a couple of days finding my way around was still sound. By coincidence, I chose to visit exactly a year after I had originally planned.

Stepping outside my hotel and on the hunt for somewhere to eat on my first evening, I was distracted by the sight of an ancient sit-up-and-beg bicycle careering down the road towards me. The bicycle was pink, surely the pinkest one ever made. Calling it merely fuchsia would have been doing it a severe disservice. But that wasn't the most noticeable thing about it. It was completely out of control, wobbling dangerously and swaying ominously each time a car passed by. As a silver Ford, going much too fast for a city centre and far closer than was safe, overtook, the girl riding the machine finally lost her balance and, handlebars swinging wildly, she collided with the kerb. I watched in horror as, in slow motion, she flew through the air, eventually crashing to the ground in an untidy heap. The bike, following after, landed on top of her. As she lay on the pavement unmoving, the driver raced away. I am not sure he even noticed what he had done.

Running across the road, I pulled the bike away, and flinging it aside, held out my hands to her.

"Are you okay?"

"Yes, I'm fine." As tears were running down her cheeks, I wasn't completely convinced.

"I grazed my knee, that's all," she continued.

I looked down. The knee, red and sore, had blood seeping from a rather large graze. It looked very painful.

"Are you sure?"

She nodded, but her head was not what was occupying me. The scraped knee sat in the middle of a very long and rather skinny leg, which poked out from an extremely short skirt at one end and finished at the other, with eight-hole, cherry-red, lace-up Doc Martens. Noticing that my attention was not where it should be, she wiped away her tears with the sleeve of a rather grubby jumper and, taking my hands, allowed me to pull her upright. She weighed almost nothing. Now she was standing, I found myself staring directly into an enormous pair of brown-flecked green eyes in the middle of which was a tiny, upturned, freckled nose. Directly into them, I realised in awe. She was as tall as me and I was well over six foot.

"Hi, my name is Elizabeth. Beth, just to stop you mistaking me for the Queen," she told me. I noticed a slight pink tinge move to her cheeks as she said it.

"Hi, I'm Richard; no relation to any royalty as far as I know."

"Nice to finally meet you, Richard." She gave me a smile that, splitting her face from ear to ear, displayed a mouthful of perfect white teeth. "Oh, and it's okay to let go of my hands."

Face burning, I tried to take them away but, squeezing them tight, she added, "If you don't want to, that's alright as well."

Taking the hint, I stayed holding on for a few more seconds before, uncomfortable about this level of intimacy with a complete stranger, I finally dropped them. To overcome the uneasy silence that followed, I picked up her bike and, leaning it against a nearby lamp post, pretended to give it a once-over, looking for damage. The bike joined a small bunch of cellophane-wrapped flowers, which were already there. *Had she dropped them when she crashed?* I wondered. As she didn't say anything, I assumed they weren't hers and left them where they were.

My check over, she took her turn in examining the bike. She gave it a more thorough inspection than me, but finally, placing it against the lamp post, she let out a long breath.

"Is it okay?"

"I think so. It's not mine, that's all. The last thing I needed was to break it. I'll probably be in trouble anyway."

Before I had any chance to reassure her, she grabbed the handlebars and marched away. With no idea what to do next, I stared after her like some drooling idiot. After a few steps, she took pity on me and, turning, asked, "Are you coming or what?" The question was accompanied by another of those smiles.

I didn't need any further invitation and, for the second time in as many minutes, I took the hint.

If she had any plan for our wanderings, it was not

obvious. With the bicycle on her right and me on her left, we strolled aimlessly. Sometimes our hands brushed together. This gave me an idea. Stay as close as possible and take any opportunity I could for our hands to touch. As, each time this happened, she showed no sign of moving away. After about the third time, I just held on. Her hand was soft in mine. It felt nice.

Until that point, she had been quiet, but with the hand issue settled, she now delivered a never-ending and breathless biography of every one of her sixteen years. The only things I remember clearly were that she had just taken her GCSEs and was awaiting the results; she wanted to be an English teacher and was good at the high jump. That last revelation didn't surprise me at all. In truth, I wasn't really listening. All I could think of was this force of nature walking next to me, and that she was holding my hand. Actually, in her more excited moments, she squeezed it as well. The only information I managed to give her was that I was starting university here in the autumn and that I was staying overnight so I could take a look around.

"I'm not doing anything tomorrow, if you need someone to show you the sights," she offered.

For the third time, I took the hint and accepted. I was beginning to get very good at it.

The invitation for tomorrow seemed to be all she was waiting for. Giving me a peck on the cheek, she climbed onto her bike and, after a few false starts, pedalled away. As she turned a corner, bike rocking alarmingly, she called back, "Outside the hotel at ten."

"It's a date," I shouted after her, but by then she was long gone. My only issue was whether I would actually be back at the hotel by then. Lost and alone in a strange town, I had no idea where to go. It took me nearly two hours to find my way back and I went to bed hungry.

I spent a restless night and, unable to wait a moment longer, was outside by a quarter to ten. She was already there waiting; her knee, still raw and oozing, had not been dressed in any way. *That's going to leave a scar*, I thought, but said nothing. What her reaction would be to such a comment, I wasn't sure, but I knew it wouldn't be good. Then I looked into her eyes, even bigger than the night before, and the knee and everything else was forgotten.

Our route around town had a Beth-type logic to it. Starting in the centre, she quickly introduced and dismissed the museum – 'dead and dusty'; the library – 'too many boring books'; the cinema – 'spotty boys trying to get inside my pants'; and the post office – 'never been inside, never needed to.' After that we moved outwards to more important matters. The takeaways the best – 'never been poisoned there'; and the worst – 'you will die a horrible death after one bite'. Finally, and most importantly, we explored the shops that would sell her vodka underage – all of them ranking equal in her praise. Every item of information was delivered in a rapid out-of-breath voice filled with laughter, jokes and slight touches. She was funny, pretty, good company and I was already way beyond smitten.

As the morning waned into afternoon, we strolled by the bank of the river leading out of town and drifted into the surrounding countryside. Soon we were walking along a high-hedged, narrow lane. No longer meandering, we moved with a purpose. Under a powdery-blue sky, we breathed in the scent of flower-filled meadows and eavesdropped on the conversations of unseen birds. If I had thought she was intense while we were in the town, I had underestimated her. She knew the name of every plant, the song of each bird and had an opinion about everything we saw or heard. Her passion was overwhelming.

"I never want to leave this place," she told me. "They will have to drag me away, kicking and screaming."

Never having been tied to anywhere or anyone that deeply, I found her enthusiasm puzzling and, at the same time, contagious. Soon I was as infected as her.

As the lane ended, petering into a gravel track overarched by massive oak trees, we walked into a wood, the gravel crunching loudly under our feet. After a couple of minutes, the track faded into a faint pathway covered inches deep in dried and fallen leaves. The trees were much closer here, quietly pushing in on us. No longer was there the low hum of traffic in the distance, even the birds had fallen silent. In fact, all I could hear was the soft rustle of the leaves we had disturbed. Now, deep inside the woods, Beth stopped and, suddenly serious, asked, "Can you keep a secret?"

I nodded. Our whole time together had been leading up to this moment, I was sure. It felt as though I was being put to a test. I struggled not to let my imagination run too wild, just in case I failed.

"Promise you won't laugh?"

"I'll do my best, but unless you tell me what it is, I cannot promise."

"Hmm, that seems reasonable." Taking my hand, she led me a little further along the path.

Without warning, we came to a small clearing. There, the bright sun dappling through the branches lit-up a tiny, postcard-perfect stone cottage. It was impossibly beautiful, a place that shouldn't have existed outside of a chocolate box top. Thatched roofed, roses and wisteria climbing up its walls and around the windows, it was surrounded by a low box hedge, broken only by a white-painted wooden gate. Inside the hedge was a perfectly manicured lawn. Stopping by the gate, Beth closed her eyes and breathed in deeply.

"One day," she told me, in a voice so low that I had to lean in close to hear, "I am going to live here and raise my family."

As ridiculous as that might have sounded from a sixteen-year-old, the seriousness with which she said it overwhelmed me. After a day of watching her getting excited over every little thing we had seen and done, the solemnity of the statement was both unexpected and moving. There was no way I could have laughed at her. More importantly, I didn't want to. I was beginning to understand how someone could love something this fiercely. Until that moment, if I ever imagined my future, I had always been alone. Now, I saw myself middle-aged, sitting in a deckchair at the heart of that lawn. Cold beer in hand, I listened as inside Beth sang songs along to the radio, while from the back garden came the shrill cries of happy children playing. I counted them.

"Three."

She didn't ask what I was talking about. She just rested her head on my shoulder and whispered, "Two boys and a girl."

Arms wrapped around each other, her head still on my shoulder, we meandered back to town in silence. All the way, my logical mind fought a losing battle with my fantasies. It was far too soon. We were both much too young. I hardly knew her. I could stay on after university. We could spend the rest of our lives together. I almost told her that I was sure I had enough money to buy the cottage. But for that idea at least, common sense won over. It was something I would tell her sometime soon, but not now.

*

At the hotel, she stayed outside while I collected my luggage. In my imagination, a slow walk to the station was followed by a passionate kiss as we parted. Not as good as what I had imagined happening in the woods, but still a nice thought. But when I returned, she had vanished. Looking up and down the road, I ran to the end, went inside a nearby shop, quizzed passing strangers, but she was nowhere to be seen. Eventually, afraid of missing my train, I went to the station alone. Her disappearance didn't surprise me, it seemed a Beth sort of thing to do.

It was only when I was in my seat and the train crawling out of the station gathered speed that my mind filled with questions. What did I know about her? How would I find her again? Other than her first name, that she had a friend with a pink bicycle and would probably have a scar on her left knee, I knew nothing. I tried to console myself with the thought that she could always find me if she wanted. It wasn't much of a comfort.

From that day on, I thought of little other than her. I

think I may have even gone a little crazy. When I got back to university, she never came to find me, so I spent the next three years alone, doing my best to forget. Largely, I succeeded. There were times, however, when I thought I saw her or imagined a pink bicycle disappearing into the distance. When this happened, I made half-hearted enquiries about her and, on a couple of occasions, even placed adverts in the local paper. There was never a response. I even considered hiring a private detective, although I backed off before I did anything about it. Even in my most insane moments, that seemed to be going a little too far. You might think that all I needed to do was to go back to the cottage and wait. Of course, you would be right, and there were many times I tried to do just that, but I never managed to find it again. In the end, I decided that it and Beth were some sort of hallucination and did my best to move on.

By the end of my course, a good degree in my pocket, I was largely mended, although sometimes late at night as I was dropping off to sleep, her voice would come whispering, "This is where I am going to live and raise my family." When that happened, the returning pain overwhelmed me and, as if it were only yesterday, I buried my face in my pillow and wept.

It was my last day in town and deciding to have a final look around, I found myself at some point standing outside the hotel. It was three years to the day since I had stayed there. Crossing the road, I stood by the lamp post and remembered that first evening. It was then that I saw them, a familiar bunch of cellophane-wrapped flowers. They were the same ones that had been there that first evening. No, not the same. These ones were fresh today.

While I had no idea why they had been left, they did give me an idea. If history was repeating itself, all I had to do was to follow my journeys with Beth exactly. If I did, I might just find the cottage and her with it. Why hadn't I thought of that before?

Hunting through the museum, libraries, post office – the cinema had closed down – more takeaways and dodgy vodka shops than I cared to remember, I was beginning to lose hope when I found myself marching along a familiar riverbank. Soon, I came to a turn-off and beyond it a country lane. At its end I discovered the old gravel track, just as I remembered it. Now all I needed to do was walk to the clearing and wait. It was then that the tiny flicker of hope that had sustained me through the last three years finally died. She wouldn't come and even if she did, she wouldn't remember me. I carried on anyway. I deserved closure.

Exactly where it had been the last time stood the cottage. It would be nice to say it was unchanged, but that wouldn't be true. While obviously the same building, the difference was alarming, far more than could be explained by three years and an overcast day. Still beautiful, it was now in need of extensive repairs: the wisteria was dead, the thatch patchy and the garden overgrown. No children had played here in a long time. Now I was no longer seeing it through Beth's eyes, it had lost its soul.

"Can I help you?"

I must have jumped.

"Sorry, I didn't mean to startle you. But was there something you wanted?"

Standing behind me was a woman of about seventy. She was slightly stooped, but in her younger days must have been very tall, about as tall as Beth. More importantly, she was holding a pink bicycle. Not the bright pink of memory. Like the cottage, it was faded and worn.

"I know this sounds stupid, but do you know a young girl who used to come here? She would be about nineteen now."

Her face fell. "Oh, you mean Beth."

My heart raced. "Yes," I stuttered. "I have been looking for her."

"I thought I had seen you here once before. I put it down to my imagination. You had better come in for a cup of tea."

I must have hesitated.

"Please do. You will need it, believe me."

While she made the tea, the woman told me that she had inherited the cottage when Beth was five. She had never had enough money to renovate it, but that didn't matter to Beth. She had fallen in love with it and from then on would tell anyone who would listen that she would raise her family and grow old there. As she got older, and had issues with her parents, she visited more and more frequently.

"And that was the problem," the woman said. "She came once too often and stayed far too long." As she said it, she wiped away a tear.

"What do you mean."

"She regularly came here after school. One evening, she popped in for a second and stayed for a chat. Then she told me that she was running late; there was a man in town who was going to change her life forever, and she didn't want to miss him. She sometimes saw things others didn't, you know. Do you understand?"

I nodded, "I think so. She must have known I was going to be there."

"It wouldn't surprise me at all. Because she was in such a rush – she always was – she asked whether she could borrow my bike. Against my better judgement, I said yes."

"And?"

I was beginning to feel uncomfortable. She was talking about her in the past tense and was now crying properly, tears rolling down her cheeks, clutching a handkerchief, chest heaving.

"I should never have let her go," she sobbed. "She really wasn't a very good rider, but she insisted. She hadn't even got to the end of the track before she came off and grazed her knee."

"I remember the knee," I said. "I assumed it happened when she fell off her bike in town."

"You were there?"

"Yes, when she fell off her bike, all she did was graze her knee."

"Beth," she said in a quiet voice, not much more than a whisper, "hit her head against a lamp post when she fell. She died instantly. I blame myself. I could have stopped her, but she was insistent. I leave some flowers there every year on the anniversary."

"I saw them there earlier." By now, I was crying as well. "But they were also there the first time I met her."

"When was that?" She seemed perplexed.

"Three years ago – to the day."

"You met her three years ago," said the woman. "Are you sure?"

I nodded. "I was meant to be here four years ago, but everything got delayed by a year."

"Curious," she said, "although I am not surprised. Something as simple as being dead would never stop Beth if she was determined." Her voice dropped to a whisper. "Beth died four years ago today. You two met exactly a year after her accident."

And then I understood what Beth had meant by 'finally'.

A STORMY NIGHT IN GEORGIA

The lights turning green, I hit the gas and passed yet another garish strip mall. This one was even brighter than the last. The highway, ramrod straight to the horizon, cut through the lantern-mooned, billiard-table-flat landscape that was so different in every way to the winding, wooded lanes of home. As a flash split the sky from west to east, I began counting. I got to five Mississippis before the low rumble arrived. I still had a little time, but not much. *Why, I wondered, when eighty-five per cent of people around here lived within two miles of what I was looking for, was I finding it so difficult to locate?*

How long had I been travelling? If you had asked, I would have told you over an hour, but my watch told another story. I had been away less than ten minutes. As I glanced again, the second hand slowed further. Now each tick lasted an eternity.

I hadn't wanted to abandon her inside that seedy sixty-dollar room. With its broken-spring bed, leaking shower and frayed, stained carpet, it had nothing to recommend it. It was the sort of place you wouldn't think to leave your worst enemy, let alone your most treasured possessions. But she had insisted and, as always, I had obeyed.

On my right, I spied a small square of run-down stores. The storm now only four Mississippis away, I signalled and turned. If I circled around and took an illegal left on the way out, I would be heading back to her. She would be left unsatisfied. I would have to live with the consequences.

Once in the parking lot, I became distracted. An eye-searing array of neon signs promised me the delights of furniture, guitars and guns. One store in particular caught my eye, offering as it did the pleasures of both liquor and hot tubs. Intrigued by the prospect of a shot of bourbon while sitting in a bath of bubbly hot water, I parked up. Perhaps, I persuaded myself, someone inside might know where I could obtain what she needed or, if not, tell me where I could find a reasonable substitute.

I never got the chance to find out. As the crack of small-arms' fire echoed around the square, I decided that being a live coward was a better proposition than being a dead hero. Slamming the car into drive, I gunned the engine. Even so, I was too late. A posse of blues and twos, lights and sirens blaring, had turned in and while they surrounded the bar, the last stopped directly in front of me, blocking my exit.

As two officers climbed out, slamming their doors and unholstering their weapons, I switched off the engine and rolled down the window. Raising my hands high, I asked, "Can I help you?"

I hoped that my obvious non-local accent would reassure them that I was harmless. If it did, it wasn't obvious and, taking an exaggerated crouching position, they shuffled towards me, firearms raised.

"Throw your keys out of the window and exit real slow," ordered one.

I obeyed.

"Place your hands on the roof where I can see them and spread your legs," commanded the other.

I did as I was told.

Only then did they dare approach. Patting me down, and satisfied that I was unarmed, the one doing the patting relaxed a little and holstered his handgun. The other, a few feet back, still had his ready and aimed.

"Could you show me some ID, sir?" the first asked with that exaggerated politeness all officials use when all they want is for you to give them an excuse to cause you pain.

"My driving licence, sorry, driver's license is in my wallet, inside my jacket," I answered.

"Take one hand off the roof and reach in."

Following his instructions to the letter, I removed my wallet and held it out between thumb and forefinger. And that's where it got complicated. At first, they struggled to identify my licence for what it was. After I told them what to look for, its line drawings of the vehicle types I was and wasn't allowed to drive really confused them. In the end, they were not satisfied until a call to HQ confirmed what a British licence should look like.

After that, with a warning that this was not a good part of town for a stranger and the instruction to 'have a nice day' ringing in my ears, I drove away. Not wanting to attract any further attention, I kept to the rules and turned right instead of my intended left. By now, I was only counting two.

Straightway I hit another red and, grinding my teeth, swore to the heavens. It helped a little, but not much. To relax, I switched on the radio where I was greeted by some country singer saying that he intended to drive all night. As this was a sentiment I didn't need just at the moment, I slammed the off button and, in the blessed silence that followed, tapped on the wheel and waited for either death or old age. Whichever came first didn't matter, I had failed.

Either side of me, drivers sat hunched and tense. Whether they were on their way home to their loved ones or, like me, were trying to fulfil a mission of mercy, I couldn't know. Regardless, through no fault of their own, they were trapped on this highway to hell and, sad at the thought of her waiting helpless, my heart went out to them as well.

*

Our flight had arrived five hours late. We should have spent the night close by the airport but, keen to reach our new home, we agreed to move on. That had been my first mistake. Within the hour, shivering and shaking, she had begged me to find us somewhere to rest. The answer of sorts – the motel, dog-eared and run-down – lay just off the interstate. Hidden behind a derelict lot of abandoned cars and ruined buildings, it held little charm, but by now anywhere with walls and a watertight roof would have done. With minimal discussion, we stopped and checked in.

As soon as we were in the room, she dismissed me, ordering me to find the only possible thing that could assuage her needs. I was not comfortable at the prospect and had begged her to come with me. She refused. By now, she told me, she was not capable of doing anything beyond lying down and resting as best she could. So, I went on my own. That had been my second mistake and now here I was, who knows where, with nothing to show for all my efforts.

To give her credit, she had fought her cravings, but with her increasing exhaustion, they had turned to a longing, then a desire and finally a hunger so fierce she was no longer in control. As the madness consumed her, full of tears and apologies, she begged for my help and I gave in. As always, I was incapable of denying her anything she wanted, however damaging it might be. *How could this so recently strong and capable woman*, I wondered, *have become so totally dependent on me to feed her increasingly bizarre and constantly changing needs?*

*

I wanted to call her. It would give her time to calm down a little before I got back. But it wasn't that simple; I had left my phone on the chipped and greasy bedside table in the room. She could have been calling me all this time and I would never have known.

As the lights changed and the next mall hove into view, I braked and drove in. Now, only a single Mississippi from the storm, I had to turn back. I was out of choices.

And then I saw it. At least thirty feet high, the immense,

brightly lit, double arch forming an 'M' was accompanied by a sign boasting: 'Over fifty billion sold'. As I slowed the car, my breathing joined it and, like waves ebbing from a beach after a high tide, my anxiety drained away.

I was not a moment too soon. As I ground to a halt beside a small, perforated metal box and pressed its button, the Mississippis dropped to zero and the heavens opened releasing their load of giant hailstones. Bouncing deafeningly against the roof and hood, everything else became inaudible.

"Large fries, large burger with cheese and an apple pie with ice cream, please," I shouted, "and can I have extra ice cream with that pie?"

"Did you say extra?" queried a bored, robotic voice, struggling to make himself heard over the din.

"Yes, please. My wife needs that extra ice cream. I won't get a moment's peace if I come home without it."

I explained my predicament and, suddenly sounding very human indeed, the speaker responded, "It's okay, sir, I understand. I have been there myself."

So, on a thundery night in Georgia, I raced the storm to find my wife and as yet unborn child their fix of apple pie and ice cream. Hopefully, once sated, they would sleep peacefully, if not comfortably, until dawn. Then, when the morning came, I would, no doubt, be expected to satisfy a whole new set of cravings. What would they be? Who knew? Certainly not me.

SKINNY DIPPING AT THE BISHOP'S

The front door slammed, and our lives crumbled. The bishop was home. As his size elevens stomped down the oak-panelled corridor, I stuffed the rags back into the bin bag, while Sandra did her best to wave away the overpowering stench of petrol. My career lay in ruins and all because of a cheap disposable lighter.

"Sorry if we are interrupting anything but, as you can see, we are back," the bishop called out, voice in full sermon mode.

"No problem at all," I replied, heaping in the last armful and nodding to Sandra to lock the door just in case he didn't take the hint. "Just tidying up after a swim."

*

And the weekend had started out so well, it really had. My friend and boss – Vincent on a good day, Vin on a really good day or, more frequently and always in front of others, Your Grace – had decided to take his family away for a few days.

"Why don't your boys come along as well?" he had said. "I'm sure you two could do with some time to yourselves."

He was right, of course, we were desperate for some us time, so we took the weekend off as well.

That had been Friday morning and now it was Sunday afternoon. All that time, we had egged each other on like a couple of giddy teenagers, rather than two very married forty-somethings. Then, almost at the last possible moment, following a lunch of flirting, Prosecco and spliffs, we finally got up the nerve and, stripping to the buff, skinny-dipped in the bishop's pool.

The love-making that followed was unplanned, but the best I had experienced in, well, forever. Now post-coital, slightly stoned and thanking God that I worked for a high-ranking official with a big house and an indoor pool, I rolled over and, lying on my back, looked up at the crumbling ceiling tiles.

Reaching out for my wife's hand, I gave it a squeeze.

"How was it?" she whispered.

"The best ever," I replied. "We should do this more often."

"What, swimming naked in your boss's pool, shagging poolside or getting rid of the kids for the weekend?"

"Any of them. All of them."

"And you don't mind the wobbly bits that didn't used to wobble?"

I rolled over and gave her a peck on the end of her nose. "I am completely enamoured by your wobbly bits," I replied, "both old and new."

Lying back and closing my eyes, I remembered the times before marriage and minors and almost wept.

These days, our intimate moments were little more than a quick fumble on my birthday. This had been our first opportunity to be alone in over a year.

A little chilly, I opened my eyes and, looking around for my robe, stopped dead. There, in the far corner, half hidden and almost invisible to anyone not at floor level, was the unmistakable slow red blink of a CCTV camera.

"Shit!" Pulling myself up onto my knees, I yanked my hand from hers and, using a small towel, the only object within reach, covered her essentials.

Disturbed by my outburst and sudden activity, but still sleepy, she turned towards me. "What's wrong?"

"There's a bloody CCTV camera filming us, that's what's wrong," I exploded.

She bit her bottom lip, something she always did when I annoyed her, an act that regularly drove me wild with desire, but not today.

"Don't ruin everything with one of your stupid jokes," she hissed.

"I'm not joking, I'm really not."

"Oh my God," she screamed and, jumping up, ran from the room doing her best to cover her modesty with what I now saw was a very small towel indeed.

Pulling on my robe, I followed her out, discovering her slumped against the hallway wall, hyperventilating. I understood how she felt. This was a very big deal indeed. While liberal-minded about many aspects of theology, the bishop was not, I was sure, the sort of person to appreciate his Archdeacon performing drug-fuelled, semi-pornographic acts in his private pool. It would be bad enough if he saw the movie himself, but what if the camera linked to some form of call centre? If that thought worried me, the one that followed was even ghastlier. Supposing one of his junior clergymen, particularly one of the more ambitious ones, had been tasked with reviewing the recordings. Within minutes, he could make a name for himself, and me for altogether different reasons, by sending the film to one of the less reputable redtops. My career would be over in an instant, either fired or, worse still, exiled to a parish in the wilds of Wolverhampton. With each new thought, my panic grew and soon I was breathing in harmony with the wife.

Taking some deep gulps, I forced my pulse to slow and did my best to focus on the problem at hand. Eventually, I came up with an answer.

"Okay," I said, flopping down next to her. "I have a plan."

She leant forward in expectation. "Congratulations; what is it?"

"We find and destroy the tape, and failing that, we burn the palace to the ground."

She groaned. "Not exactly well thought through, is it? Of course we need to destroy the tape, but we cannot torch the place."

"Why ever not?"

"First, because the bloody camera will film us doing it, and second, because I used the last two matches lighting the, you know. You know what I mean."

"I hadn't thought of that," I said.

She rolled her eyes heavenward. "Well done, Einstein."

We sat in silence for a few more minutes while I grasped for other options. "Alright," I said eventually. "A new plan. We confess and throw ourselves on Vincent's mercy."

As soon as the words left my lips and her mouth dropped open, eyes widening in horror, I knew that my new idea was, if anything, worse than the first.

After a few moments, she replied, "The first plan it is then. We have nearly six hours before Vin returns and if we haven't found the tape in the next four, we get some matches."

Slowly and deliberately, I nodded. "It's a deal."

So began our game of real-life Cluedo. Sandra, using a screwdriver, tried to break into the bishop's office, leaving in her wake a deep-seated gouge that could never be eradicated from the ancient oak door frame. While she was doing that, I followed the cable from the camera to the point it disappeared through the wall and into the garage next door. Unfortunately, the garage was locked and the key was nowhere to be found. *No problem*, I thought, *I can get in through the skylight.* All I need is a ladder.

Halfway up, after several near catastrophes and while wondering when the bishop had last been forced to climb a ladder, I managed to put my foot through a windowpane. The good news was that I was now able to open the skylight with ease and, crawling inside, I hung from the frame before dropping to the floor.

Picking myself up and dusting myself down, I walked over to the point where the cable should have appeared from the other side, to find nothing. No wires came into the garage, either there or anywhere else as far as I could see. Disappointed, I unlocked the door from the inside and went in search of Sandra.

With few other options, we decided to widen our search. Looking for a secret chamber, we knocked on the panelling in the library until our knuckles were raw. *Might the wires have gone upwards instead of across?* we wondered. We shifted our quest to Vincent's bedroom where broken floorboards and grubby Persian rugs soon lay piled on his bed. Of the recording device there was, of course, no sign. We placed glasses against every wall in the hope of detecting the sound of whirring machinery and, with all other options eliminated, we used high-intensity, electromagnetic radiation to erase the tape from a distance. Well, we would have done, had we had any idea what it was and how to do it. Everything we tried failed. We couldn't find the bloody thing anywhere.

With only two hours left, we admitted defeat and reluctantly put the second part of our plan into action.

"You go home," I told her, "and get some rags. At the same time, find some hose and drain petrol out of your car. There is an empty can in our garage. While you are at it," I continued, "I will pop down to the corner shop and buy some matches."

By now, she was way beyond words and did nothing more than roll her eyes. As she walked across the lawn towards our smaller but much-loved cottage, sitting in the shadow of the cathedral, I shouted after her, "Don't forget to pack a change of clothes. We will need them once we are on the run. Actually," I added, "it might be a good idea for you to get dressed at the same time. You won't get far naked."

She carried on in silence and had I not seen her shoulders slump, I might have thought she hadn't heard.

Our local shop is only five minutes' walk away, but I decided to drive. Even so, I was too late, arriving just as the owner flipped the sign from open to closed. Running to the door, I banged on it, soundlessly pleading with him to open up. The bastard, making no effort at all, tapped on his watch and, smiling, walked away.

"I hope that the flames of hell consume your goolies for all eternity, and even then, you will be getting away lightly," I mouthed, almost crying in frustration. But with his back to me, he missed the entire curse.

Now what should I do?

There was a petrol station on the bypass, I remembered. It would be open and was only five minutes' drive away. I could still do this.

So, I returned to the car. Finding it locked, I patted my robe – had I really come here without getting dressed? – but my pockets were empty. *Think, man, think. You must have had the keys with you when you left and when you got here, otherwise how could you have driven or locked the car?* The distance between kerb and shop was less than thirty feet, so there was no way they could get lost, unless – *unless* – they had fallen into that drain right underneath the driver's door.

On hands and knees, I peered down and there they were. Squeezing my fingers through the grating, and skinning my already-sore knuckles, I did my best, while all the time cursing my builder's hands, so stubby in comparison to Sandra's pianist fingers. As hard as I tried, I just couldn't reach. Another inch was all I needed, but it was an inch too far.

Getting my hands stuck would do no one any good, so, after one last try, I sat on the kerb and did my best to think of another solution. Surprisingly it came and the answer was so simple.

Going by road wasn't the most direct route to the garage. Across the field was. If I ran, I could be there in ten minutes tops, say another five buying the matches and then fifteen getting home. I could be back at the palace in half an hour. I still had time.

Halfway across the field, for once empty of cows but unfortunately not their excretions, reality hit me. While I might have been able to run this distance in ten minutes some twenty or so years ago, dashing across a muddy field in rapidly fading light wearing nothing but my robe and Sandra's pink fluffy slippers was a completely different prospect. Not being the sort of person to countenance failure, however, I kept going, arriving at the garage a mere fifteen minutes later. Gasping for breath, sweat gushing from every pore and doubled over in agony as the stitch gripped my side, I placed my hands on my knees and wheezed, "A box of matches, please."

"Any petrol?" asked a neanderthal, locked behind a security screen.

"No, just the matches."

"Don't do matches."

"How about a lighter?" I panted.

"Fifty pence," he replied. That was better. I reached for my wallet, the nice brown leather one that Sandra had bought me for my last birthday. The one that was now resting happily on the passenger seat of the car.

It was then that I lost it. Sobbing like a three-year-old, I sank to the floor and, curling into the foetal position, I screamed obscenities while kicking against the counter front. Sandra's now-ruined slippers slipped off and I stubbed my toe.

While my wailing failed to awaken even the slightest semblance of humanity in the moron behind the counter, it worked perfectly for the elderly lady parishioner watching from the safety of the newspaper section. As I slid into complete hysteria, she, brushing imaginary dust from her flowered hat, adjusted her horn-rimmed spectacles and, stepping over me, placed a fifty-pence coin on the counter. Then, taking the cheap disposable lighter offered in return, my stalwart of the Women's Institute solemnly leaned down and handed it to me. Turning, she walked out of the garage. She never uttered a word.

The attendant joined her in that silence. I guess he was just relieved that this nutter would soon be out of his shop.

It took me another twenty minutes to get back to the palace, arriving a dishevelled, broken wreck. However, I was, it had to be said, a dishevelled broken wreck with the means to commit arson.

Shaking, I knelt beside the petrol-drenched rags. "Shall we do this?" I asked.

Without a word, she bowed her head in agreement and I clicked the lighter. Nothing! I tried again and this time was treated to a spark followed by the merest hint of flame. It lasted for less than a second and as it guttered and died, I pressed for a third time. The lighter disintegrated in my hand.

"What sort of mindless fool sells broken cigarette lighters?" I screamed.

"I don't know, but I do know the sort of idiot who buys them," she answered. "Now what are we going to do?"

"Don't worry, I will think of something."

There was no time to get back to the garage, but we still had a good half hour. *Will there be matches anywhere in this non-smoking household?* I wondered. Or is it really possible to light a fire simply by rubbing two sticks together?

It was then that the bishop arrived. That was all the motivation I needed. And as we piled the rags back in the liner, my mind stepped up a gear and there it was, the answer. It was so obvious; it was a miracle that I hadn't thought of it earlier. Unlocking the door, the only obstacle between us and the bishop, I did the only thing one could decently expect from a red-blooded Englishman. Opening it, I thrust Sandra through and slammed it shut behind her.

"You tell him."

I relaxed. She had nowhere to go, no escape. It was down to her to explain and make a clean breast of it. I winced as the pun hit me.

On the other side of the door, I could hear her shuffling footsteps and, after what seemed an eternity, the low murmur of her voice.

The bishop's response confused me, however. Apoplexy? No. If anything, it sounded more of a giggle; a giggle that rapidly evolved into something altogether noisier. I might have been mistaken but it sounded like a series of almost manic guffaws. I could almost imagine his portly frame shaking from head to foot. But why?

Then the door crashed open. Face burning, shame and anger written all over it, Sandra pulled me through and, pointing to the bishop almost doubled over in delight, screamed at me in a voice cold enough to freeze hell itself, "They are fakes; every camera in the whole place is a dummy. They don't work, they never have, they never will and if you hadn't made me tell him, he would never have known."

LOST HORIZONS

I woke in Lhasa just as the first cock crowed. Struggling to see clearly in the weak half-light, I realised that I must be losing my sight. Worse still, as I tried to climb from my narrow mattress-less cradle, hot pokers shot through my every joint and I was forced to sit back down. In this dream, I had grown old.

As the light strengthened, my cataract-clouded eyes discovered an ornately carved walking stick that had not been there on my previous visits and, grasping it tight, I pushed myself upright. Leaning on it heavily, I persuaded my arthritis-bound body to climb the roughly hewn stone steps that led to the wide-open eastern terrace.

By now, the sun was showing itself over the snow-covered mountains and as dawn raced towards the city, I heard, but could not see, the black-necked cranes hooping as they made their way across the morning sky in search of breakfast. At that moment, faint on the breeze, came the aroma of bread frying in innumerable kitchens in the city below. My mouth watered. I was very hungry indeed.

A slight clearing of the throat made me turn and there,

as he had been in every other dream, was Mr Zopa. Unlike me, he was unchanged, looking exactly as he had the day he disappeared from his chippie in Newcastle.

"Good morning, my friend, and how are you today?" I asked.

As always, Mr Zopa bowed deeply and said nothing as he held out the fresh *balep* and, as I inhaled, the smell of scorched barley took me back to the back room of Mr Zopa's on the mist-shrouded banks of the Tyne.

This time I woke for real, still in my bed in Nan's terraced house. Mr Zopa and his family had been missing for over a year.

*

My first clue that the day was not going to be a regular Tuesday ought to have been the exotic sand pattern someone had drawn on the pavement outside our house. A mandala, I was later to discover. The second, had I bothered to pay attention, should have been the two saffron-clad monks sitting in the Sunday room with Nan and Mr Zopa. Being eight, I ignored them all and, discarding my school bag, grabbed a Garibaldi from the biscuit tin on the sideboard. Switching on the TV, I sat down in the living room and watched yet another repeat of *Bagpuss*.

"Billy, love!" yelled Nan. "There are two gentlemen to see you. They have come all the way from Tibet."

If I was impressed, I wasn't going to show it. A visitor from Tibet was no match for the stray dog that had got into the Ross's house last week and pooped all over their brand-new carpet. It had been the only topic of conversation all the way to and from school ever since. Switching off the TV, I ruminated on the subject of Tibet. Even if I had heard of it, I certainly had no idea where it was. Somewhere over the river near South Shields, I guessed.

Mooching into the Sunday room, I discovered two robed men sitting at the dinner table while Mr Zopa and Nan sat in the comfy armchairs. Left with little choice unless I wanted to sit with the two strangers, I placed myself, hands behind my back, in front of the empty fireplace and, red-faced, stared down at the carpet. This was the position I always took on my frequent visits to the headmaster's office. I was a little confused though. How had I managed to offend these people so badly that they had come all the way from Tibet to complain about me? Not knowing what the best way forward might be, I decided to keep quiet.

After a long and uncomfortable hush, it was Mr Zopa who finally broke the ice.

"Hello, Billy, as neither of these two gentlemen speaks any English, and I speak Tibetan, they have asked me to translate for them. They need some help and want to ask you some questions. Are you okay with that?"

Not sure what to say, I shuffled my feet some more and carried on staring at the floor, hoping that a portal into some other dimension would open up and take me there. As it quickly became obvious that this wasn't going to happen, I gave him the briefest of nods. After all, it would be rude not to help if I could. Especially as I was pretty sure I hadn't done anything that either of them could be really mad about.

Taking my nod as a sign that it was alright to carry on, one of the monks picked up Nan's best tea tray from the table. It was covered with a brightly decorated cloth.

"The gentlemen would like you to tell them what is on the tray?" said Mr Zopa.

How am I meant to do that while it is covered up? I wondered, but, unusually for me, I kept my mouth shut. If they wanted to play games, what was wrong with me having some fun? Screwing up my eyes, I pretended to look hard, so they would think I was trying.

Then something strange happened; the cloth became as clear as a polythene bag. Beneath it, I could see five objects.

"There are five things," I told them. "A pair of rimless glasses, some beads tied into a loop with some sort of coloured string, a scarf the same colour as the clothes you are wearing, a wooden spinning top and…"

I couldn't see the last object clearly. I knew it was there but had no idea what it was. As I spoke, Mr Zopa translated. The monks stayed silent. I screwed up my face even harder, the fifth item was turning out to be a bit of a problem. Every time I tried to focus on it, it squirmed out of sight behind the other objects. I broke into a sweat and the back of my shirt became wet as it ran from my neck and down my spine. Droplets sprang out on my forehead. This was ridiculous; why was I allowing myself to get into such a state over an old flip-flop?

That was it; I had finally cornered it at the edge of the tray and, unable to escape, it had showed itself.

"It's an old sandal," I said, "but there is something wrong with it. It isn't like the rest of the things. It doesn't belong."

I opened my eyes to find everyone staring at me. Whatever I had said, I had obviously been wrong. Mind you, that was hardly surprising; I am not Superman with his X-ray vision. Then I looked at the now-uncovered tray. On it were five objects exactly as I had seen them: a pair of glasses, some beads, a scarf, a spinning top and, finally, an ancient leather sandal. Mr Zopa gave me a reassuring smile and, pointing at it, asked the monk a question. As I couldn't understand a word of what he was saying, I assumed he was speaking Tibetan. The monk raised his leg and waved a bare sandal-less foot at Mr Zopa, whose face broke into a broad grin. He had amazingly uneven teeth.

"You were right, Billy; the sandal did not belong. Thank you so much for being so helpful. I need to talk to your nan some more. Why don't you go back into the other room and watch TV?"

It was about ten minutes later when Mr Zopa put his head around the door. Nan was with him. I was in the middle of watching some other repeat so didn't pay them too much attention.

"Billy, why don't you and your nan come down to the chip shop after school Friday? Some friends of mine will be visiting. There will more than enough chips for everyone. Also," he added, as an extra inducement, "Elvis will be there." Now I was listening; I never ignored an opportunity to spend time with Elvis.

And with that, he stood aside as the two men came into the room. Placing their palms together as though they were saying a prayer, they bowed to both Nan and me. Then, before they left, the older one draped a thin white scarf around my neck. *What a funny way of saying goodbye*, I thought. After I had seen them out and closed the door, I went back into the Sunday room. Nan was sitting in her chair, crying, and I had to give her a hug and make her a cup of tea to get her stop. I didn't ask what was wrong. Something deep inside told me that I didn't want to hear the answer.

*

Just in case you were wondering, Elvis is a stray ginger tom who adopted Mr Zopa the day he and his family moved in. Mr Zopa called him Elvis because a scar on the corner of his mouth makes his lip curl into a sneer, just like the real thing. Elvis is unwavering in his snarling hatred of anything human except, for some reason, me. Whenever we meet, this spitting ball of fury becomes a playful kitten, rolling onto his back and purring so loudly that people in the street turn their heads wondering what the noise is. I think he does it to encourage me to tickle his tummy. He tolerates Mr Zopa and his family only, I guess, because they keep him regularly supplied with fish. Everyone else in the area, including the dogs, wisely cross the street to avoid him. I'm telling you all this just in case you thought I was talking about the other Elvis. I wasn't, of course, because, as everyone around here knows, he works at the Maccy D's in the Metro Centre. Elvis is not the only link between me and Mr Zopa. He took over the chip shop the very same day I went to live with my nan.

*

Friday was a long time coming, and all week I had trouble sleeping, my dreams disturbed by high snow-covered mountains and fluttering flags. That evening, getting home from school, Nan insisted that I put on my best clothes and shooed me out of the door.

"Aren't you coming, Nan? You were invited."

"No, Billy, I think it's best that you go on your own. It's a decision only you can make."

What decision? I wondered as I walked towards the chip shop, idly kicking stones. It seemed unfair that I had to make choices about things to do with saffron-clothed Tibetans. It didn't make any sense. Mind you, nothing had since the day they arrived.

When I got to the chip shop, the door that was normally fixed open was closed tight. That was strange. Fridays were Mr Zopa's busiest evening. Something must be seriously wrong for him to shut up shop. I was about to leave, when I saw a sign on the window. It said that the shop was closed for a special event. Using my sleeve, I wiped the rain away from the window and peered in. It wasn't very easy to see because the inside of the glass was so steamed up, but it looked like the place was full. I could see Mr Zopa and his family, as well as the two monks. There were also loads of other people that I didn't recognise. All of them were standing around chatting in an uninterested, waiting-for-something-to-happen sort of way. Not knowing what else to do, I knocked on the window and Mr Zopa, smiling, rushed to let me in.

"Hello, Billy. You are to be our guest of honour tonight. Let me introduce you to everyone."

Before he had a chance to do any such thing, Elvis –

the cat, not the singer, obviously – sidled up and, hissing at everyone to stay away, rubbed up against my shins. As I squatted down and stroked him behind his ears, he rolled onto his back, presenting his tummy for a tickle. After a few minutes, seemingly satisfied, he got up and wandered away, presumably in search of fish. I looked up. The room had fallen silent, and everyone was staring at me.

As soon as I stood up, I was overwhelmed. Everyone wanted to talk to me all at once. The strange thing was that although none of them were speaking English, I could understand every word they were saying. Even more extraordinary, I didn't seem to be speaking English either and they seemed to understand me.

Eventually Mr Zopa rescued me and, taking me over to the counter, dished me up a big bag of chips and scraps. Not for the first time, I noticed the poster of an immense white-and-red building stuck to the wall behind him. *The Potala Palace*, I told myself.

How had I known that? A gale blew through my head, and I remembered other people who had lived there, some of them hundreds of years ago. The thing is, they all seemed to be me. Then I understood and shivered. That was what this evening had all been about. I had lived there before, and they wanted me to live there again. I didn't like that idea one little bit, I can tell you.

"The palace has been your home for over six hundred years," said Mr Zopa as though reading my thoughts.

"No," I insisted. "Here is my home."

He nodded half-heartedly. "I understand how you feel. Let's go into the back room and talk."

The back room behind the shop is tiny. It is where Mr

Zopa and his family stay when they are not serving chips. The two monks were already there sitting at the cramped dining table and as I walked in, they got up and bowed to me, doing that prayer thing again. I knew exactly what was going to happen next; they were going to try and persuade me to go with them. I wasn't going to let anyone talk me into doing something like that. As anyone who knows me will tell you, I am normally quite easy to persuade, especially if someone wants me to do something stupid. But not this time; I was not going to leave Nan on her own. Without giving them any chance to speak, I said, "I can't go. I need to stay here and look after my nan."

Mr Zopa had no need to translate; from the look on their faces, it was obvious the monks understood. For a while we sat in silence, no one saying anything. I had expected them to try and persuade me, but they didn't, although they did appear sad. Eventually, Mr Zopa got up and, with a sigh, said, "Just stay here for a little while, Billy, while I talk to the people outside." He walked into the chip shop, leaving me alone with the monks.

After what seemed an absolute age sitting in embarrassing silence, Mr Zopa came back and, ignoring the monks, said, "Come on, Billy, let me take you home."

Leading me through the now-empty chip shop, he walked me back to my nan's.

*

The next day, Saturday, I played footie with my friends. When i got home, there was a surprise waiting for me. Sitting on Nan's lap, purring his socks off, was Elvis.

"Mr Zopa brought him round. He thought Elvis might want to stay with us for a while."

I didn't need to be told what that meant.

"Sorry, Nan, I've got to go. Back in a few minutes." And with no time to say anything else, I ran out of the door and headed up to Mr Zopa's.

I was, of course, too late; the chip shop was all boarded up, looking for all the world as though it had never been open in the first place.

But as I turned back home, out of the corner of my eye, I saw, attached to a part of the door where no one could easily see it, a small triangle of fabric. On it, in Sharpie, someone – Mr Zopa, I assume – had written: *Next time in Lhasa, Billy.*

*

As Nan tucked me in that night, I gave her a big hug. "I'm glad that's all over," she said. "I want to forget that the last few days ever happened."

I said nothing. It wasn't going to be that simple. I knew I had done the right thing by staying to look after Nan, ably assisted by Elvis, but I couldn't help feeling that I had let everyone else down.

It's been fourteen months now. Mr Zopa and his family never returned, and no one has ever mentioned them. It's as though they never existed. The only evidence of them is Elvis, that tiny piece of cloth hidden safely in my bedroom and my nightly dreams.

It was not long after he left that I came to understand that Mr Zopa and his family arriving the same day I moved in with Nan was no coincidence. He and Elvis had been sent here to watch over me and keep me safe.

These days, my every dream is haunted with visions of Tibet and meeting Mr Zopa again. Someday soon, the call will become too strong to resist and, when it does, I will have to leave home and embrace my future as a lama. As Mr Zopa whispered in my ear that night when he dropped me off after the gathering at the chip shop:

"One day, we will meet again, Billy. The next time we do will be in Lhasa."

I have known for quite a while now that my nan will be safe here with Elvis looking after her and that there is no real reason why my 'someday soon' can't be today. *Why not?* I ask myself every morning as I look in the bathroom mirror. And just like every other day, I give myself the same answer: *Because you are too scared to face your destiny.*

THAT MOST MAGICAL OF FRUITS

The unprovoked and simultaneous attacks on the USA, China and Russia by the Andorran Federation, the newest of the nuclear powers, brought a unified response that was both swift and brutal. It left the tiny Pyrenean province little more than a smoking, radioactive ruin. While the number of people killed by the saturation bombing was surprisingly small, the impact of the fallout and the subsequent nuclear winter spreading across the continents of Europe, Asia and eventually the Americas was catastrophic. Over eighty per cent of the plant-food species were wiped out. Had it not been for the global seed vaults located on the Svalbard archipelago, largely undamaged during the complete elimination of the polar ice caps, it is unlikely that humanity would have survived at all.

What amazed everyone, though, was how quickly the earth regenerated itself. Mind you, it was hardly surprising given the amazing reduction in carbon emissions and microplastic disposal. The rapid regrowth of the natural environment after the Chernobyl nuclear disaster ought to have provided some clues, perhaps.

In all the chaos, and then hope, there was one plant that bizarrely resisted all attempts of reintroduction: the humble banana. With its limited gene pool arising from generations of selective breeding by those seeking to grow larger straighter fruit, it had little ability to adapt to the rapid changes in its environment. Within a matter of years, the plant no longer existed outside of major botanic gardens such as Kew in West London. At first, the loss of this children's favourite, although much lamented, made very little difference to the day-to-day life of the average person beyond a fleeting sympathy for the now unemployed and destitute banana pickers of the tropics. Unbeknown to us, however, this delicacy, as it turned out, was the key to mankind's long-term survival.

*

No one was sure exactly where or how the contagion started, but within months this highly communicable and always-fatal disease had spread from the Pyrenean dead zones to the major European population centres and then on to Asia and the Americas. The distances involved hardly slowed its progress and soon people on every continent, regardless of gender, age and race, were falling victim to its deadly embrace. Starting with a slight cough, within days the sufferer experienced excruciating arthritic pains that no known analgesics could relieve. This was followed by an extended and painful decline as the internal organs and finally the brain degenerated into a slimy mush.

With no one sure of its origin, it was assumed that radiation was the cause. It soon became obvious, however, that this was not the case as uncontaminated locations such as New Zealand and Antarctica became as badly infected as the more-tainted regions.

As humanity succumbed to this mysterious virus and care services across the world collapsed, people dropping in the streets were left unattended due to a combination of fear and a lack of suitable burial places. Millions died and unless a cure could be found, it seemed that mankind was doomed.

*

I struggled from my bed. This morning I felt a little better and, wrapping myself in a blanket, I sat by my bedroom window and watched the sun rise over the Thames. Emotions dulled by pain and increasing infirmity, this part of the day was the only pleasure left to me. *I am pathetic*, I thought bitterly. Until three months ago, I had been a sprightly fifty-year-old, running five kilometres every morning along the unpeopled banks. Now, like so many others, I was prematurely aged: broken, brittle and palsied with nothing to look forward to excepting an early and agonising death.

I clenched my fists. This was no time to feel sorry for myself. I still had much work to do before the disease violated my brain, leaving me a drooling, gibbering wreck. As soon as I had stopped quivering sufficiently to dress, a chore that now took me over an hour on a good day, I made my way across the few yards of lush grass that separated my prefabricated apartment block, built to house the regrowth scientists, and entered the laboratory.

When I first got the job, I travelled into town by train, but once I became sick, I was offered a place in the apartments, even though I was not doing anything directly to rebuild the world. At least what I was doing, however small, was a help, I told myself and I will keep working as long as I still have the strength to sit at my desk.

While not a trained mathematician, I have always had the ability to spot patterns in numbers. Someone had apparently told somebody else that I might spot things that others missed. Within weeks, I was assigned to the insignificant project of looking for clues as to how it might be possible to save the banana. Each day, I was emailed masses of number strings. I did little more than stare at them looking for patterns in the plant genome that the AI computers had failed to identify. While they were excellent in what they did, occasionally, albeit rarely, a human with the right skills and a bit of intuition could spot something they had missed.

Arriving at my workstation exhausted, I lay my head on my desk for a few minutes. For the last week now, I had had to do this to recover from the exertion of the short walk from the apartment to the laboratory. Each day, the time I needed to recover was becoming longer.

I must have dozed off. Suddenly, I became aware of a distant voice calling my name.

"Eve, wake, up, I've got something wonderful to show you." I recognised the soft voice of Adam, one of the plant scientists.

Reluctantly opening my eyes, I almost fainted in amazement. There, in front of me – yellow, too tiny to be real, almost bent double but for all that perfectly formed–

Adam had placed... Yes, it was a banana, apparently the first to grow naturally in nearly twenty years.

"That pattern in the data set you spotted a few months ago gave us the clue we needed to regrow them," he continued.

I looked at the yellow fruit, so much smaller than I remembered, and salivated. "A banana, oh my God, how I've missed them."

"Go on, give it a try," Adam whispered. "I have a whole bunch. Now they are finally growing again, there seems to be no stopping them. If anyone deserves to eat the world's first post-apocalyptic banana, it's you."

Gingerly reaching out to what seemed a mirage, I picked it up, peeled back the skin and sank my teeth into its soft flesh. My first mouthful of my favourite fruit in such a long time. It tasted so good. Just like eating a summer's day.

As I chewed, something strange happened, and as I swallowed, a tingle that spread outwards and downwards from my mouth surged through my entire body. As the chemical tsunami faded, it was replaced by something else. Nothing at all. The pain that pervaded every pore of my being had gone. I gasped.

"What's wrong?"

"My pain, it's gone."

I wriggled my fingers and toes and then moved my neck around in circles. Something I had been unable to do for weeks. Yes, it had definitely gone. I pushed myself upright and, standing unaided, I waved my arms around.

"Look, Adam," I said, turning, "I can move."

There was no reply; he had gone. Rather embarrassed,

I sat back down, wondering what to do next, and when nothing else came to mind, I got on with my day's work. Not for long, though; within minutes, Adam was back with a bunch of medics, and I was rushed to the medical centre. For the next three hours, I was prodded and poked, had blood taken, was scanned, and those were the tests I recognised. All, it appeared, to no avail. By the next day, the pain had returned and by that evening, I was feeling no better than I had before. That was not the point though; one small banana had alleviated my symptoms for a whole day.

Within months of my providential discovery, untainted volunteers who were fed a diet of nothing but bananas had developed an immunity sufficiently robust to allow scientists to create a vaccine. In trials, the results were miraculous. It rapidly stopped the spread of the disease and, if the organ damage was not too far advanced, it aided the recovery of those already afflicted.

It was too late for me, however. While a diet of now freely available, albeit expensive bananas helped relieve the pain, the destruction of my system was too far advanced for there to be any hope of recovery.

*

On a cold winter's day, just over a year after my breakthrough, I sat on my favourite bench in the middle of my beloved Kew. Wrapped in a blanket, I watched as a woodpecker daintily hopped across the frozen ground in search of worms. It was, I knew, one of the last times I would see such a thing. I did my best to feel sad at the prospect but failed. It was probably time for me to go.

As I sat there, I became aware that some people, wearing white coats and carrying clipboards, were walking towards me. As they were obviously something official, I did my best to stay awake for them. For several days, I had found it more and more difficult to remain conscious for more than a few minutes at a time. But before they arrived, my eyes drooped and, slipping from the bench, I fell to the ground. Waking mid-fall, I saw them running towards me. For some reason though, when they got to me, I was floating, looking down at them and me. A very strange sensation indeed.

"Such a shame," said one. "Today of all days; the first time the vaccine has been available to everyone on earth, and she didn't live to see it."

"Not a shame," said another – Adam, I think. "She was sitting on her favourite bench in the place she loved more than anywhere else in the world. It seems a fitting way to go."

BUSTER

"Hey, you! Get out of here. Now!" screamed the large lady, her face as red as a tomato.

The shop fell silent, and I looked down at the floor. My toes, peeking out from inside my brown leather sandals, wiggled up at me. They were no help at all.

Running through my list of shopping rules (regulations, directives, mandates, commands, dictates, decrees, commandments, stipulations), I tried to think of what I had done this time. I was sure I hadn't rearranged any of the shelves in colour or size order. Neither could I remember dancing around the aisles or singing the 'Mahna Mahna' song at full blast. That last one was the main reason why my big sister wouldn't come shopping with me anymore. I had told her that I would keep my mouth shut and I had succeeded most of the time, but it wasn't long before she found another excuse not to go with me.

"How many times have I told you not to tell my friends that they have spots?"

"But they do."

That had been the last time. Now if I wanted to buy anything, I had to do it alone and look where that had got me. I had broken some rule or other and I was getting shouted at. It was so unfair; the one I had broken this time was apparently a new one that no one had told me about.

I raised my head and watched through slitted lids so no one would notice I was staring.

"Rude," my sister had told me.

Tomato Lady was now chatting to the customer at the counter, talking fast, staring and pointing. I made myself as small as I could and as the queue moved, I obediently shuffled forward, my mind whirling, wondering what I should do? My only hope was that Tomato Lady would forget all about me by the time I got to the front. If she hadn't, she might yell again. My teachers did that all the time, so it didn't bother me much. What would be a problem was if she wanted to throw me out. To do that she would need to touch me. I don't like being touched, especially not by grown-ups. If people touch me without asking, I get angry and become a bit of a pickle. When I am a pickle, people start shouting and lock me in a room until Mum comes to collect me. Then she gets mad, not with me, but with them and she starts to cry, telling them that I am a good boy really. When she does this, I have to put my arms around her and promise that if she stops crying, I will never be a pickle ever again. We both know that this isn't true because I can't help it.

The queue shuffled forward again, and now I was at the front. I was shaking so much at the thought that the Tomato Lady might touch me, my tummy tightened. That really scared me. Sometimes when my tummy gets tight, I wet my pants, and I didn't want that to happen in the shop. So, before she had a chance to say anything, I ran, moving so fast that no one could catch me.

Outside, it was raining and, pulling my hoodie over my head, I looked around for somewhere to hide. It didn't matter if I got wet. Getting wet in the rain doesn't break any rules. It's only getting wet when you jump in the river that does. I had jumped in several times, which had started the new rule: don't jump in the river with your clothes on. This didn't worry me that much; it was easy to keep. So, the next time we were at the river, I just took off my clothes before I jumped in. My sister's friends all screamed, and she told Mum, so now I am not allowed near the river at all. For some reason, though, getting wet in the rain is alright.

I wandered round the back of the shop. I had explored there before and knew that during the day it was empty. It only got busy when the shop closed. First, they took out all the rubbish, then, much later, my sister and her friends met up with boys and kissed them and smoked cigarettes. But for now, it was deserted, so I sat and thought about what had just happened.

Pulling my notebook – an A6 black, lined hardcover one; the one I take with me everywhere – from my jeans pocket, I looked at my list of shops. This one hadn't been open long, I remembered. I had written its name in my book the day it did. I was pretty sure I hadn't been in there. If I had, I would have remembered, but I decided to check anyway. Sure enough, there were no dates and times or what I had bought written down, just the name and an opening date written in big capitals. I added today's date and the time, followed by a little cross to tell me that I had been asked to leave. Normally, I added the reason as well, but as I didn't know, I wrote down a '?'.

I became aware that I was being watched. This happens to me a lot, so I sort of have a sense of it. Doing my best not to panic, I looked around in a nonchalant sort of way so that the watcher wouldn't know that I had noticed them. Regarding me from a few feet away was a rather scruffy patchwork dog. He had grey paws, an inside-out ear and was licking his lips in a rather self-satisfied way.

"Hello. What's your name?" I asked.

He didn't answer but came up and sat down next to me. I scratched him behind his ears. Leaning his head on my knee, he sighed. It's what Mum does when I have broken some rule or other once again. As we had only just met, I assumed that he was sighing about someone else.

Had he been a person, I would have definitely become a pickle at this point, but as he was a dog, I felt that it was okay that he didn't ask permission to touch me. Anyway, as I hadn't asked whether it was okay to scratch him behind his ears, I couldn't complain. I like dogs; it's people that are my problem.

"I'm going to call you Buster," I told him.

Buster gave a little whine of disappointment and shifted himself again, knocking over the bottle of fizz sitting between my knees. It was the one I had been about to buy when I ran out of the shop, the one I was sure I remembered leaving on the counter. My blood ran cold and, squeezing my eyes shut, I wished it gone. But on opening them again, it was still there. Now, as well as a pickle, I was a thief.

Doing my best to breathe, I tried to think of what I should do. The first thing that came to mind was to go back into the shop and explain that my stealing had been an accident. But what if they didn't believe me and they threw me in jail? I had seen jail cells on TV; no windows and no room to dance. In there I would always be a pickle, and every time Mum came to visit, she would cry. At that thought, my eyes began to prick and soon tears were rolling down my cheeks. No, I couldn't risk going back to the shop.

Buster must have known that something was wrong and, whining some more, he came up close and licked away my tears. To say thanks, I reached down and scratched his tummy. He seemed to like that, as he gave out a little moan. It calmed me down as well, which helped me think. If they hadn't come looking for me by now, either they hadn't noticed that the drink was missing, or they couldn't be bothered to follow me. That was the answer. If I never went near that shop again, I would be safe. Even so, right at the back of my mind, I was worried. I knew what I had done was wrong and so did Jesus. My stealing had made him and his angels cry. That was what all this rain was about.

By now, it was raining really hard. Although, to be honest, it didn't seem to bother Buster that much, I was getting very wet. I decided that it was time to go home and get dry before I caught a cold.

Getting up, I put the notebook in my pocket and whistled to Buster to follow me. After thinking about it for a few seconds, he got to his feet and, shaking himself dry, walked after me. It was nice having a friend. Perhaps

I should ask Mum whether he could stay with us. I was sure that my pocket money would be enough to feed him. He could sleep in my room at night so he wouldn't need a kennel. Having a dog would be great; we could go on long walks together and he could jump in the river, even though I wasn't allowed.

Just before you get to the street where I live, there is a main road. It has a place where you press a button and wait for a little man to turn from red to green. When that happens, it's safe to cross. As we waited, I told Buster my plan.

"I'm going to ask Mum whether you can come and live with us."

He shivered and, turning around, ran back towards the shop.

"Come back," I yelled. "You don't have to be Buster; you can have any name you want. Just come and live with us, please."

But he ignored me and was already so far away that I am not sure whether he even heard me. Then, the man changed colour. *Of course*, I told myself as I crossed the road, *it wasn't being called Buster that was the problem, it was the thought of living with my family.* I understood where he was coming from, especially if he had already met my sister.

*

In the kitchen, I thought about Buster and the good times we would have had together. It made me feel sad that I didn't have a dog. Then I remembered the drink. What should I do with it? Supposing the people from the shop came looking for it, then what would happen?

I needed to get rid of it, but how? Obviously drinking it would be the easiest thing to do, but that would be wrong and would make my crime so much worse. I felt guilty all over again and every time I looked at the bottle, it got worse. Not knowing what else to do, I hid it in the fridge and went into the other room to try and forget. Not being able to see it helped, but not for long and very soon, as hard as I tried, it was all I could think about. Supposing one of my family saw it in the fridge and drank it? Then they would be a thief as well and it would all be my fault. Perhaps it just being in the house was enough to make my whole family criminals.

While the idea of my sister being locked away was thrilling, the thought of my mum in prison made my eyes prickle again. The only thing to do was to hide the bottle away from the house, somewhere no one would find it. Fortunately, I knew just the place.

Taking it from the fridge, I went out into the garden. At the end, as far away from the house as you can get, is an old, nearly falling-down shed. Because its door is hanging off, and half the roof felt is missing, it lets the rain get in, so no one other than me goes there. Right at the back, underneath some grotty mouse-bitten sacks, is a loose paving slab. I saw it wobble the first time I went in to watch some mouse babies, all bald and blind. Underneath is a place where I bury all my treasures, stuff like my special stones and some old medals I found in the loft. Things I don't want anyone else to know about. Things that if my sister found them, she would laugh and throw away.

She has done that with my special stones before. I hid the bottle there.

*

Mum always tucks me in at bedtime and asks about my day. This evening, there was nothing I felt I could tell her, but she obviously knew something was wrong.

"What is it, darling? You have been quiet all evening."

"Nothing. I'm fine," I told her.

She didn't say a word but looked at me in the way she does when she knows that I am lying, eyebrows drawn together, and mouth turned down. People have told me that mothers always know. Mine certainly does. I did my best to outstare her but eventually, face burning, I looked away.

"Tell me about it," she said, voice gentle. And through my tears, I whispered about what had happened in the shop, confessing to everything except the stolen drink and Buster. In the silence that followed, I held my breath and waited. I knew what was coming; she would hug me, tousle my hair and tell me that everything would all be alright. Most of the time this felt good, but tonight I needed something more, a solution rather than comfort. That was never going to happen in this household of women, but for once I was wrong.

"So, before you ran out of the shop, you hadn't broken any of the rules."

"No, I really didn't. Unless there are some new ones I don't know about."

"Let's walk through them."

I told her.

"That all seems fine," she said, "well done." She paused for a moment and then said, "I don't think that you are telling me everything. Are you?"

And with nowhere to go, I told her the smaller of my two secrets, holding my head against her as I sobbed my confession.

"What you did wasn't right, but I understand you must have been very frightened. It is not nice to be shouted at, especially when you have done nothing wrong."

"What should I have done?"

"You should have gone straight back in and told them that loud noises scare you and that is why you ran away. Then you could have offered to pay."

I shook my head. "But they would have sent me to prison."

"I know it seems like that, but that wouldn't have happened, darling. It would have been fine. And you know that is what you must do."

I shuddered. "You do it for me."

"I can't do that. It has to be you. But I don't think it needs to be done tomorrow or anytime soon. Why don't you promise me that one day, when you are feeling brave, you will go back and explain. Then you can offer to pay."

I nodded, but I was sure it would never happen.

*

I was wrong for a second time, and five days and ten minutes later, after three failed attempts, I finally plucked up the courage and went back into the shop. As a way to begin the conversation about my crime, I picked up another bottle of fizz. Holding it in my right hand and clutching the exact money for two bottles in my left, I joined the queue. As everyone shuffled forward, I practised what I would say. By the time I was nearly at the front, I only had a few butterflies left flying around my tummy.

It was the same lady at the counter, but this time she didn't seem so angry. She wasn't tomato-coloured anyway. I was still frightened of her though and started to shake. Then I remembered the professor in the *Harry Potter* films who tells people to take the scariest thing they can imagine and turn it into something funny. Although the lady wasn't a tomato, she was still large and rather pink, so I pretended that she was Miss Piggy. It made me feel a bit better.

I was only one place away from the front of the queue, when who should wander through the door but Buster. Sidling up to the cold cabinet where they keep the meat pies and pasties, he calmly helped himself.

As Miss Piggy saw him, she turned scarlet and screamed at the top of her voice.

"How many times have I told you? Get out of here. Now!"

Buster ignored her and, leaving her stuck behind the counter, helpless, he left the shop in his own good time. It hadn't been me the woman had been shouting at. It had been Buster all the time.

Then I knew what I had to do. Keeping hold of the bottle and putting the money back in my pocket, I ran out of the store as fast as I could, chasing after him.

Outside, round the back, I found him snapping and

pawing at the cellophane covering a meat pie. Picking it up, I tore it open and, breaking the pie apart, fed it to him in small pieces. While he was still licking the last of the pie from his lips, I sat down and, taking a big slurp of the drink, I belched loudly. Buster, obviously approving of what I had done, covered me in slobbery kisses and laid his head on my lap. I scratched him behind his ears, and he let out a soft moan of pleasure.

"What do we do next?" I asked.

I didn't need him to answer; I already knew what our future held. We were going to lead a life of crime, heading up a gang of desperate international criminals. It was going to be amazing.

THE LETTER

Supposing one overcast April morning your doctor told you that you had less than three months to live. What would you do next? Grab some paper and write a bucket list, possibly. Gather your nearest and dearest and tell them your news, probably. Not me. I sat down in the surgery reception area, pulled out my phone and booked the first available flight to Venice. Given the time of year, it seemed the only sensible thing to do. What happened next? That's what I am about to tell you.

An hour later, after collecting my passport and wallet from home, and picking up a prescription of industrial-strength painkillers from my local Boots, I hit the M25. There were many other things I ought to have taken, such as a guidebook or a change of clothes. The reason I hadn't, you might believe, was because I wasn't thinking straight, understandable under the circumstances. It's not true though, my real reason was much simpler. I wanted, no, needed, to travel without baggage, either emotional or physical.

It never occurred to me that such a lack of luggage

would be problematic. In that I was wrong. There is obviously something deeply suspicious about a middle-aged man travelling abroad with nothing but keys, wallet and drugs to accompany his passport. At the airport, I was subjected to several rounds of questioning and a rather more thorough search than I found comfortable. My explanation that I was dying and wanted to see the canals before I was the wrong side of the grass didn't convince anyone.

Beyond security, I decided that it might be wise to change my plans a little. After all, I didn't want the same experience at the other end. Also, with the best will in the world, the emotional baggage was going to come with me regardless.

Amongst the myriad of shops in the terminal, one seemed the most appropriate, relatively inexpensive and casual. Inside, I bought two pairs of straight-leg jeans – size thirty-four standard length; five pairs of underpants – medium; the same number of socks; and three plaid shirts – large. As I stood in the queue to pay, a thought hit me. Arriving at the other end with nothing more than a paper bag full of clothes might be just as suspicious as carrying nothing at all. So, leaving the queue, I hunted for some sort of suitcase, eventually deciding on a large leatherette rucksack. Not only was it big enough to hold my new wardrobe, but it also left me with some space for anything else I might want.

Purchase complete, I headed towards the nearest toilets and, locking myself into a tiny and rather odorous cubicle, I stripped. In the cramped space it offered, that was not an easy task, believe me. A couple of pulled muscles and a bruised elbow later, I had managed to discard my old life and, now resplendent in my new ensemble, I went to put on my shoes. In my search for everything else, I had forgotten about shoes. The ones I had with me, leather and formal, were completely unsuitable, I decided. Abandoning the cubicle, I bundled my old clothes, along with the shoes, into a waste bin and padded back to the shop in my stockinged feet. The bad news was that they only had one pair in my size. The good news: they were rather comfortable hi-top trainers. All the better for exploring the streets of Venezia.

My grand plan for simplicity now in tatters, I went into the chemist and spent some money on a toothbrush, toothpaste, a comb and some deodorant. I decided against shower gel and shampoo, as obviously a bathroom in any reasonable hotel would already have those. The hotel. In my rush, I hadn't booked anywhere to stay.

"You really should have thought things through a little more thoroughly," I scolded myself.

Still, I had twenty minutes before boarding, so, using fifteen of them, I booked a room. Not the Danieli as originally planned, but still a nice, albeit much cheaper place in the north of the city. I spent the remaining five minutes buying a guidebook. I was sure that I wouldn't need one. After all, I had spent the last fifteen years assiduously studying the layout of the city in the ancient Baedekers that lay gathering dust on my bookshelf at home, but, you never knew, they might have built a new canal.

As the plane crossed the still snow-covered Alps, I came to the conclusion that I had made the mother of all mistakes and the best thing to do would be to catch the first flight home.

Unable to do anything about it for the moment, I did my best to relax and watched as we passed the glittering, shimmering snow of the mountains. Unfortunately, as always happens when I am distracted, my mind turned to her. Heartbroken I might be, and as understandable as that was, knowing that I would never meet and love anyone again still hurt. As usual, I wept. Fortunately, I was used to covering up such things and apparently no one noticed.

As it turned out, getting home wasn't going to be as easy as I expected. Instead of going back to the UK, my plane went on elsewhere and there were no further flights home that evening. I was stuck in Venice for the night.

For the first time in ages, I slept soundly. So much so that by the time the dawn broke bright, I had dismissed all thoughts of returning and decided that now I was here I might as well make the best of it. I certainly wouldn't be coming again.

Shortly after ten, following an excellent breakfast, I stepped into a bright Venetian morning. As the sun warmed my skin, so different from the English rain I had left behind, I toyed with the idea of just wandering the streets soaking up the atmosphere. But, deep down, I knew that wasn't an option. I had no choice but to go along with her original plan. Perhaps if I followed it to the letter like some sort of incantation, I might finally heal.

Keeping to the route meant that I arrived at our first stop at twelve on the dot. Enjoying the warmth, I sat outside and ordered my first of hopefully many ice-cold spritzes. As the sun sparkled on the teeming waters of the grand canal, my phone buzzed. It wasn't that anyone was trying to contact me, I had abandoned family and friends years ago. It was just that, for fifteen years now, I had set my phone alarm to go off every year at this exact date and time, the moment when we were meant to stop for our first drink of the holiday, at this café by the Rialto.

As always, when the reminder sounded, I went back to the day my life went to hell and, allowing my anger to take over, I ground my teeth and hunched my shoulders. How could she have treated me that way? At the very least, she could have let me down gently.

*

The evening before we were due to leave, I had left work early, packed and was driving over to her place, ready for an early morning start, when she called me.

"Can you pick up a takeaway for three?" she asked. "There's someone I want you to meet."

As this was a time for celebration, our holiday, I called at the best Chinese in town before heading over to her.

He was younger than me, tall, slim, everything I wasn't. His only saving grace was his obvious embarrassment at the situation. We ate our meal in uncomfortable silence, all of us aware that there was something unsaid. I ate very little.

"Let me take the plates away," she said eventually. "Then we can talk."

"I'll help," he offered.

They both disappeared into the kitchen, while I waited and waited. Eventually going to join them, I found the door slightly ajar. On the other side, they were kissing and he had his hand inside her blouse.

Unwilling to confront them, I went back into the living room and waited some more.

"Is there something I need to know?" I asked, keeping my tone light, when they finally emerged.

She told me that she had recently started working with him. They had become lovers the day they met. Unhappy about her going away with me, he had asked her not to go. While she thought his request reasonable, in the end she decided that rather than cancel, a better approach would be to change the booking to his name. Throughout her explanation, he just stared red-faced at the carpet. I guess it meant that he didn't have to look at me.

Her justification finally over, I stood and, placing the currency I had collected only that day on the table, I walked out. Her last words, even now, still ring in my ears.

"I will pay you for the tickets and hotel, I promise."

She never did. Unable to face going home, I spent the night crammed uncomfortably on the back seat of my car, wondering why I had let her do this to me.

*

Things had to change, I decided, as I took the first sip of the recently delivered bitter, orange-tinted drink. I couldn't allow what little time I had left to be wasted sunk in this melancholy. Once more, I decided to fly home. It was time for me to leave her and this benighted city behind forever. Taking a deep breath, I let my anger fade and, as I did, I became aware of my surroundings again.

The café was buzzing. Gondoliers from nearby piers arriving in pairs spoke such rapid Italian that their words merged into a single continuous hum. I was fascinated and became so wrapped up in watching and listening that I barely noticed when someone joined me on the bench. With room for three or four each side of the rough-hewn wooden table, it was obviously made for sharing. Even so, I resented the intrusion, especially as the person had chosen to sit so close that our bodies touched. I did my best to ignore them, but when a hand began to stroke the inside of my thigh, I found that a little difficult. Lifting the hand away, I looked up at its owner and was trapped in the gaze of a pair of storm-grey eyes, encircled by the blondest of blonde hair. She smiled, a beam so warm that it could thaw the coldest of winter's days and, with that, what was left of my rage melted.

"Hello, you. It's about time."

I struggled to speak and, even after a considerable pause, all I could manage was, "Hello to you, too!"

I could have kicked myself. How many times had I planned this moment, and all I could come up with was hello. Pathetic.

"What do you mean it's about time?" I continued.

"I knew you would come eventually."

"It might have been better had you written."

"It's not quite that easy."

"Oh yes, the other man."

"Don't be like that. Bitterness doesn't suit you. Anyway, he's long gone."

"Then why?"

She ignored the question.

"Let's go for a walk," she said. "I'll make sure you know everything before it's time for you to leave. That is," she paused, "if you decide to go home at all. I stayed."

"I've missed you," I said.

Damn, how could I be that stupid. At the very least, I deserved the opportunity to be screaming and shouting abuse. Instead, I allowed her hand to fall back onto my thigh. This time, it landed a little higher than the spot it had rested on before.

Before I had a chance to enjoy the touch, however, she stood up and walked away. At first, I stayed behind just watching. Had she aged? She hadn't but she was changed. Faded might be a better description. Her hair had lost its brightness and her eyes their glow. Mind you, it had been fifteen years; it was hardly surprising.

She stopped and, turning, beckoned me to follow her. Even after all this time, she was still the only woman for me. As I caught her, she placed her arm through mine and leant her head against me. Her hair was damp on my shoulder. It also had a slight curl to it. It always did that if she didn't dry it properly.

"I've missed you too," she replied and, placing her lips against mine, she kissed me as though we had last met only yesterday. She tasted of the sea; salty and wild. It left me gasping for breath. Pulling back, she hitched up the narrow strap of her sundress, which had fallen from her shoulder. As she did, I caught the briefest glimpse of a breast, pale and translucent. I immediately stiffened, wanting so much more.

We spent the rest of the day exploring the city. The only change to the original plan was her surprising reluctance to travel on the waterbus; instead, she demanded we walk everywhere. Strange, the *vaporetto* was something that had formed a major part of our original plan. Oh well, we could always catch one tomorrow.

The day was magical, the sky clear, the breeze warm, the company perfect and as the sun set over the lagoon, we walked hand in hand through the narrow, darkening streets. As night fell, swirling mists swallowed the city, muffling every sound other than the echo of our footsteps. We could have been the only people abroad and we took full advantage of it. Each time we came upon a small, deserted alleyway, we crept inside and stole a kiss.

At the last corner before my hotel, I pulled her to me. Her body, so warm and inviting all day, was now icy in the evening air. I shivered. Not just from the cold but also from desire.

She drew away. "Sorry, not yet."

"When?"

"Soon. Perhaps tomorrow. Once you know everything. Then, if you still want, we can be together."

I felt my face redden; she wasn't alone. Even now, she was lying. Despite everything she had said, she was still with him. I turned and ran as fast as I could.

"Please, trust me," she called out. "I will explain everything. Just give me time."

I stopped. Even now, bent double, chest heaving, hands on knees, I was unwilling to make a scene.

"Okay, tomorrow then."

We didn't need to agree where. It would be in the original plan. But she was no longer there. The street was empty except for the lingering scent of salt and sea. Then, as if coming from the stones themselves, I heard the echo of her voice on the breeze.

"At ten."

And for the first time that evening, I heard a sound that was not us. In the distance, the bells of St Mark's tolled midnight and the day turned. As it did, I felt at peace for the first time in years, a peace that was soon replaced by hope. Only a few more hours and I would see her again, and then, she had promised, we would be together.

*

The Caffé Florian sits on the long side of the poorly named St Mark's square, with its back to the grand canal. Arriving ten minutes early, I found myself a seat under cover to protect us from the promised rain, and looking out so that I could keep watch for her. As I sipped my rather scalded espresso, I watched as the early lines to the Doge's Palace started to build. The visitors were marching single file along a raised metal gantry, which allowed them to avoid the remains of the winter's floods. A visit had been on yesterday's itinerary, but there being so much to share, not the important stuff as it turned out, we had decided not to waste time in the queue. *Perhaps today*, I thought.

Exactly on time, she strolled into the piazza and headed towards me. Today, she was definitely faded, the overhead clouds bleaching all colour from her. Again, her hair was curling. Once more, she had not bothered to dry it properly.

I waved and, spotting me, her face lit up and as it

did, the sun breaking through the clouds joined her and everything was perfect once again. Stopping suddenly in the middle of the square, forcing a group of tourists to step around her, she turned on her heels and walked away. Throwing notes and coins onto the table, I ran after her, catching up just as she left the square as it joined the Piazzetta dei Leoni.

Without a word, she placed her arm in mine, just as she had done the day before, and led me away. I didn't need to ask where we were going; I knew exactly.

It should have taken only ten minutes or so, but in the end it took us well over an hour. In all that time, she said nothing. In answer to all my questions, she either just smiled or kissed the tip of her finger and placed it against my lips. In the end, I gave up and allowed myself to enjoy her touch.

The Acqua Alta bookstore, as you may know, is rather unique. Cramped, crowded and home to a clowder of stray cats, the books are displayed in tubs, on raised shelves and, in one case, an ancient gondola. They have been stored this way since flooding in the early twenty-first century destroyed most of their stock. The intention is to keep the volumes dry should another flood or unplanned high tide occur. Whether it would work, I have my doubts.

I went to go inside. She hesitated.

"I don't think I can go through with this," she said. "The crowds."

"But you were going to tell me everything."

"Yes, and I will. I promise."

She seemed pale. No, pale was not the right word; by now, she was rather – how can I put this? – translucent.

"If you go inside and ask, there is an envelope with your name on it. It will tell you everything you want to know."

The jealousy returned, the joy of only a few seconds ago melting into rage. "You really are a piece of work," I shouted and walked inside.

The shop was dark and airless. Books old and new were crowded into every corner and piled to the ceiling, in danger of imminent collapse. There appeared to be little order, with the customers wandering around in a daze while looking for the books they wanted. In reality, most of them seemed to have come inside for little more than the experience and to buy nothing other than postcards and fridge magnets.

I walked up to the service counter. "*Lei parla inglese?*" I stuttered. "Do you speak English?"

"A little," a broad Brummie accent replied.

"You're a long way from home."

"Studying at the Guggenheim for a few months," she answered. "Can I help?"

"Hopefully. This may sound stupid, but is there a letter with my name on it waiting for me?"

"I'm not sure. If I knew your name, it might help."

I told her and she frowned.

"I don't think so, but it does ring a bell. Let me ask the manager."

Ignoring the queue building up behind me, she locked the till and wandered over to a man trying to explain to an American lady that the shop really wasn't built to accommodate someone wheeling a full-size suitcase around. As the girl approached and pointed in my direction, he abandoned the woman and hurried towards me as fast as the crowds would allow.

"*Signore*. You are enquiring after a letter?"

"Yes, I was told that there was one waiting for me."

"*Si*, and you have something to identify yourself?"

I pulled out my passport and, after looking at the identification page, he walked to the till and, leaning underneath, pulled out a large leather-bound ledger. Opening it to a page marked for the day, not the year, he removed an envelope and passed it to me.

"Here you are, *signore* perhaps you could answer me one question?"

"If I can, yes."

"Why have you waited so long?"

"So long – what do you mean?"

He glanced at a pencil scrawl on the envelope. "This letter was given to us fifteen years ago to the day."

"Fifteen years? I only found out about it this morning."

"As I said, *signore*, strange." And he handed over the envelope.

*

The Acqua Alta is separated from the Longa Santa Maria Formosa, the street on which it lays by a small square or rather oblong, also filled with stranded boats, second-hand books and harried tourists. It is ruled over by yet more stray cats.

Standing in a corner to avoid the pressing crowds, I was in two minds whether to even read the letter. Perhaps I should just throw it away and head home. But I had invested far too much of my life not to get to the end now, so, tearing open the envelope, I pulled out the letter, written in her familiar spidery script.

Hello, my darling. If you are reading this, you are obviously in Venice and thinking about me. That is wonderful. I hope you are remembering only the good times.

Not at the moment, I thought.

After less than two days, the letter continued, *I am here on my own, thinking about how stupid I have been and what might have been had we visited here together. It was something I always dreamed of. I am so sorry. Everything tells me to come to you and try and make everything alright but, knowing that this is impossible, I have come up with a different plan.*

I don't know how long it has been between me writing this and you reading it, but it is my intention to come here every year at this time and go to all the places we should have visited together until, I hope, we meet again.

All my love.

I looked up. It came as no surprise that she wasn't there. I ran to the end of the square, my heart pounding. I couldn't have lost her again but if she was close by, it was impossible to tell. There was no way I could spot her amongst the hustling crowds of tourists. Once again, I caught the faint scent of the sea. Then I knew what the letter meant and, sitting down on a bench, I wept.

*

"*Signore*, you are back, as I expected."

"The lady who left this letter for me. What happened to her?"

From the same page of the ledger, he brought out a yellowed newspaper clipping. Translating it slowly and hesitantly, he explained that after leaving the shop, she had caught the *vaporetto* to the Lido. Halfway across, she climbed the barrier and jumped.

"The water there, it is not very deep you understand, but there are currents. People leapt in after her, but there was nothing anyone could do."

It was then that the walnut-sized intruder in my posterior thalamus called out for attention, burning through my brain, down my spine; its message arriving as needle-sharp stabs in every extremity. At the same time, my whole body burnt like the fires of hell. Had it not been for the manager's strong arm, I know I would have fallen amongst the books, causing who knows what damage.

Customers and tourists forgotten, the manager and his assistant led me to an ancient leather Chesterfield at the back of the shop. Taking one arm each, the pair helped me to sit. While he remained with me, she left, returning a short time later with a glass of water. After I had taken a sip and had pulled myself together a little, the manager asked, "I am sorry, *signore*. The lady, she was important to you?"

It took me a little time to think of how to answer. "Very. We were meant to visit here together a long time ago. It all went wrong and she came without me. It is only now that I have got up the courage to visit."

"And you finally met her again?"

I looked at him. My eyes must have shown surprise. He smiled.

"The beautiful, sad lady, she visits us every year. I think that no one other than me sees her, but I always know when she is here."

"You don't seem shocked."

"In a city as old as this, it is not unusual for there to be visitors from the past."

I nodded. I knew what he meant.

I don't know how long I sat there, but eventually the pain subsided enough for me to move and by then I knew what I had to do. As an expression of my appreciation and also because I knew I would need them in a few minutes, I bought a branded notebook and ballpoint. Then, thanking them both for all their help, I asked for directions to the nearest *vaporetto* stop.

As soon as I was outside, I sat in the sun and wrote down everything that had happened to me since that fateful evening and what I planned to do next. Placing it in an out-of-the-way corner near the shop entrance, I headed for the waterbus.

Thirty minutes later, clutching a small bunch of flowers, I had boarded a *vaporetto* and was on my way to the Lido. The day, so warm only an hour ago, was now gloomy. A deep mist had rolled in from the sea and by now it was so thick that I could see little beyond the immediate bow wave. The *marinai*, however, seemed unconcerned, his only concession to the conditions being the occasional sounding of his siren. Not dressed for such weather, I soon became chilled and shivery.

As close to halfway as I could picture, I stood up and

slowly made my way to the barred gate meant to stop people getting off while the waterbus was still moving. When no one was watching, I silently threw the flowers over the side. At that moment, a wave hit and I lost my balance. Had a hand not grabbed my shoulder, steadying me, I would probably have gone overboard. The hand now slid down my arm and linked its fingers with mine. Body close, and hair blowing in the breeze, she gave me a broad smile.

"It's time to decide. Can you think of any reason to go home?"

I shook my head. "No, I would just sit alone, counting the days."

"Good, then let's be together forever."

A second, more violent, wave hit us. This time, she made no attempt to hold me. As I tumbled over the barrier and into the water, the screams of the passengers following me, she jumped in as well.

"I made a mistake," she whispered. "Forgive me."

She entwined her body in mine and as the water closed over my head, I took in a deep lungful of ice-cold water and nodded that I did. Then, before the water took me completely, I smiled. After all these years, I was finally happy.

A TALE OF FORTY-SIX

I sighed and, laying down the quill, rubbed the top of my nose between inky thumb and forefinger. I probably left a stain to match the many littering my arms, clothes and face.

In the almost dark of the guttering candle, I could hardly see the parchment. My head pounded. One more verse and then I would finish for the day. If I didn't stop soon, it would be difficult to find an open ale house, let alone one with food.

Oh, how I hated this work; it was just like working in a…what was the word? I couldn't think of one, but what sounded right? Factory – that was it, a good word. I might use it at some point. I smiled; I loved the way my mind worked. If I couldn't think of the right phrase, I just made up some nonsense or other– the first thing I could think of. The results were curious; people just seemed to accept whatever I had written as being genuine. Take 'arouse'; I had dropped it into *Henry VI* for a bet with Marlowe, and within weeks everyone was becoming aroused in their everyday speech.

A knot tightened in my stomach. Poor old Kit, how I missed him. As usual, when I remembered him, other less welcome feelings came pouring in and, as hard as I tried to stop it, a jealous rage overtook me. His words would still be spoken and respected millennia hence, whereas mine were unlikely to even outlive me. I finished the verse, another of a never-ending list of begats.

This was dire; how could I transform this turgidity into something that would inspire the people who read it? But this sort of pomposity was exactly what the Committee for Truth liked. Prose with any spirit whatsoever being ruthlessly exorcised, so afraid were they of offending the King. They seemed to take great delight in removing any expression of personality from the text. They wanted everything to sound as though it came from the same quill. The quill of the committee.

Forgetting my earlier vow, I tidied up another verse. Now, it really was time to finish before I lost my mind. I was organising my inks and paper, when I felt the slightest movement in the air. The candle flared and the papers fluttered. Looking up, I saw the cadaverous form of Bancroft and I shuddered. A visit from the Archbishop of Canterbury never brought with it any good news, but this late at night, the prospect disquieted me immensely.

"Master Shakespeare." His voice softened, immediately raising my suspicions. "Just the person I was hoping to meet."

'Who else were you likely to meet in my chambers?' I was tempted to say but held my tongue. Placing yourself on Bancroft's wrong side was not conducive to a long and healthy future.

"The King has a favour to ask," Bancroft continued. "He has requested a reading, for him and his court, on tomorrow's eve. Part of his St George's Day festivities."

He paused.

"There is nothing suitable in the King's new Bible that his majesty has not already heard." Throwing a bundle of papers down on my desk, he continued, "But we do have these, recently delivered from the scholars. Perhaps you could work your magic on them."

He winced. Any mention of the dark arts was potentially deadly under this monarch, and even a simple slip such as this could cost him his job, if not his head, had anyone overheard. Perhaps he now owed me a favour. I tried my luck.

"Absolutely impossible, my lord. As you are aware, I'm sure, it is my birthday tomorrow."

I did not add that I intended to spend all day and most of the night in any tavern that would give me credit.

"Also, even if I work my magic," damn, I had lost my advantage, "as you know, it takes at least three months to get anything approved by the committee."

"You fail to understand, Master Shakespeare, Will," his voice becoming conspiratorial, "we do not have time for such niceties. In this instance, the committee is irrelevant. The King commands and we obey. You will begin work immediately and will read for their majesties tomorrow evening at seven."

So, he wants me to read to the King, very clever of him. If the King doesn't like it, I lose my head. If he does, Bancroft takes credit for employing the country's leading playwright to deliver the show. There was nothing to be gained by arguing, so I shrugged, adding, "As you wish, my lord."

With Bancroft gone, I reviewed the pile of scholars' rough translations with little hope. But near the bottom, there was one that could be matched to my needs. It must have been placed there by divine providence. It was not, it had to be admitted, the greatest piece of prose I had ever read, but it held promise in so many other ways.

The day of its reading and its position in the overall testament were perfect and it did, I had noticed, contain two words that, if I took care, I could bend to my will. I read it through a second time and then a third. As I did, my chest tightened and my breathing quickened. I could make this work.

Authors and playwrights, some of the best in the land, had been employed to turn the basic translations of the scholars into an easily read style and I, along with everyone else, had tried to put my mark on the work. None had succeeded, until now that was.

I read the piece for the fourth time and, on coming to an end, I paused, eyes closed, breath held for a full two minutes, trying to imagine the finished work. Then, taking a deep inhalation and pursing my lips, I sharpened my quill. Dipping it deep into the jet-black ink, I began to write. As I rewrote the forty-sixth psalm, the bells sounded out midnight. It was St George's Day, my birthday. I was now forty-six.

Working through the night, the words came slowly at first, but as dawn approached, I gathered pace, and they began to flow. It was important that I got this right; every single word had to have its precise place, or my plan would come to nothing. Either its meaning would be lost or, worse still, its intent obvious. While this was never going to be my best work, no *Troilus and Cressida* here. If I could escape detection, my words would be recorded forever, locked into the greatest book ever written.

I finished just as dawn broke and after resting my eyes for a few moments, I began my revision, reading through every word, slowly and carefully. By the time I arrived at the end, my sense of delight overwhelmed me. I had done it. With any luck, I had tricked the committee, Bancroft and the King. Clenching my fists in elation until my grimy broken nails dug deep into my palms, I shouted my hallelujahs to the heavens. My work was flawless.

I counted again just to be sure, and my stomach clenched. A single word was out of place and for the first time in ages I experienced nagging doubts about my ability. But now, years of experience came to the rescue; I knew exactly what was needed of me. Drawing on my rapidly diminishing reserves of energy, I shrugged my aching shoulders loose, took three deep breaths and became so still that to the casual observer I might have been asleep. I don't know how long I stayed that way, frozen, before the answer came and I knew what had to be done. Sharply exhaling, I opened my eyes to the brightening spring morn and, picking up my quill, I dipped it into the ink and crossed out a single word. I had finished and now it was perfect.

I read the psalm again, this time out loud. It had a nice opening, even if I say so myself, but the first verse did little more than draw the listener in, lulling them into a false sense of security. The important word came in the third verse, the forty-sixth of the psalm to be precise: *shake*, the beginning of my name. I carried on. If I had counted right and removed the correct superfluous word, then there was even better to come. Going to the end, I counted backwards to where I had edited part of verse nine, to include the word: *spear*. In mounting excitement, I counted once more just to be sure.

Slamming my fists on the desk, I screamed out in joy. Forty-six words from the end of the forty-sixth psalm, on my forty-sixth birthday, I had found a place for the remainder of my name. Regardless of the fate of all my other works, I would live inside the King's bible for eternity.

GONE

By now, I was so used to the pull on the finger, the one where my ring lay, that I no longer paid it any attention. On my left, my tiny daughter was ever more persistent in demanding my attention. On the other side, the boy was engaged in a long and detailed explanation of how his recently acquired truck, one of those ones that metamorphosed into something else, could be transformed into a robot. He shouldn't have been able to show me. He had been given strict instructions not to open it until we got home, something he had ignored the moment we left the toyshop.

The sermon, interspersed with appropriate sound effects, was being delivered in that slow, solemn way of his that, from the moment he could speak, he reserved for people who failed to match his towering intellect. That is to say, me or, to be brutally honest, everyone else on the planet. Even now in his forties, I still have to resist a desire to run and hide when I see him gearing up to tell me how my arguments are, at best, inadequate or more likely just plain wrong.

The three of us were in a large department store the Saturday before Christmas. You know the day I mean, the one where the entire population of the city crushes itself into a single shop, seeking that last, perfect present. I can't remember why we were there. Doing the same thing, I guess.

This was not the ideal place for a lone father with young children you might think and, of course, you would be right. But then, as anyone who knows me will tell you, thinking things through has never been my strongest point.

My still-ignored daughter was becoming increasingly persistent, until she wasn't. Becoming aware of the lack of tug, I looked down. 'Keep hold, I don't want to lose you in this crowd or I will never find you', I went to say, but she wasn't there.

Boy kept talking.

I scanned the heads of the crowd for several seconds. What a stupid idea that was. Looking at heads would get me nowhere; she was, after all, only three. I looked at feet instead. She wasn't there either.

Boy had finally stopped talking. Now, his wide brown eyes looked up at me as his legs jiggled wildly.

"I need the toilet."

That was all I needed. Irrationally, I became angry with him. If it hadn't been for his incessant chatter, this would never have happened.

"For once in your life, please shut up. You'll just have to wait."

His eyes filled with tears and a single large drop rolled down his right cheek.

"I don't think I can," he sobbed.

I did my best to ignore him, calling out her name again.

Surely she has just wandered off somewhere, I told myself. *If I go back to the entrance, walking past all the pretty, bright, sparkly things that distracted her on the way in, not to mention the smelly ones, I will find her.* I retraced our path through the store. She was still nowhere.

By now, people were staring at us. Me rushing around, him crying and agitated. A few asked whether I was okay.

"I've lost my little girl."

"I'm sure you will find her soon," said one.

"Find a shop assistant, they have a system to find lost children, just in case," said another.

Just in case of what? I wondered. Then the fear hit. What if… It began as a swirling crater in the bottom of my stomach, soon transforming itself into a lump in my chest and then a paralysing mist of confusion in my brain.

Next to me, the boy was now wriggling uncontrollably. I breathed deeply and held it in. It helped a little. As some measure of clarity arrived, I knew that the first thing I needed to do was to sort him out.

"Can you hold on until we find your sister?" I asked. "Can you wait that long?" The look on his face told me that he would try his best, but it was unlikely.

Squatting down, I spoke as gently as I could. Upsetting him any further was not going to help.

"I need you to be really grown up. Can you do that for me?"

He nodded.

"The toilets are just there. I need you to manage for yourself."

He nodded again.

"I need to go and look for your sister while you are in the toilet. When you have finished, you just stand outside and don't move an inch. Do you understand?"

He nodded for a third time.

"I will come and get you as soon as she is safe." Damn, I shouldn't have said that, but he hadn't noticed.

Excited at his newfound responsibility, he ran as fast as he could towards the men's room.

As I watched him go, I kept my fingers crossed that he made it in time.

Now he was sorted, at least in the short-term, the fear returned. This time, however, it was much deeper. My heart raced, a pain gripped my chest; my clothes were wet from the cold, cold sweat that was penetrating everywhere.

With no other option, I decided to involve the store.

I approached a nearby assistant, but just as I went to speak, another shopper distracted her with some inane question about opening hours. While I waited to get her attention, I reverted to a middle-aged, middle-class and oh-so-British man. What if she was just hiding? What if she had left the shop altogether? I would look a complete idiot. Embarrassed, I turned around and searched yet again.

Boy had not appeared from the toilets.

Finally, with no other options, I went back to the same assistant. She was now unoccupied.

"Excuse me, I've lost my little girl. I can't find her anywhere."

"How long has she been missing, sir, and how old is she?"

"Twenty minutes, perhaps longer, I don't really know. I have searched everywhere. She is three."

"And her name?"

I told her but kept talking. I always talk too much when I am frightened.

Holding up her hand to silence me, she quickly and efficiently turned her attention to a walkie-talkie. She gabbled some words I didn't understand before turning back to me.

"You should have come to us sooner. In situations like this, time is of the essence. But don't worry, we will find her. We have a procedure, and it works."

She turned back to the crackling radio. I was not really listening, but every so often the odd phrase cut in.

"Close all doors except the main entrance."

"Identify every child leaving."

"Search the toilets."

"Make an announcement on the Tannoy."

"Does she have a pet name?" Now she was talking to me.

"Pumpkin," I replied. "But don't you need to know what she looks like?"

"Not relevant, sir; they may have changed her appearance. New clothes, cut her hair. She may look like a boy by now."

Changed her clothes, cut her hair, what on earth was she talking about? She was lost, mislaid, misplaced. Surely she hadn't been stolen, abducted, kidnapped – or worse.

"What do you mean?"

"Just covering all our options, sir."

It was then that I remembered the boy. I looked over at

the toilets; he was still not there. He had obviously ignored my instructions and now I had lost them both.

Then, over the shop assistant's shoulder, I saw him. Not a little boy, but a guardian angel disguised as a five-year-old. Gap-toothed and smiling from ear to ear, he was sitting on the top of a large pile of Chinese rugs, waving at me with all his might. Meanwhile, his left arm was wrapped protectively around his little sister.

She, of course, was paying him no attention at all and was entirely focused on sucking a Mars bar that some kind passer-by had gifted her. Its caramel core was spread across her face and clothes while her hands were covered with its, now-melted, chocolate coating. And as I watched in horror, she absentmindedly wiped her mucky paws clean on that oh-so-expensive Chinese rug.

A MESSAGE FROM THE PAST

I have always said that when your phone rings at three on a Sunday morning, it can never be delivering good news. This is especially true if you work for a bank, and you are on the fiddle. Taking a deep breath, I picked up the phone and was, of course, proven right. On the other end was the bank's auditor and he wanted to see me urgently.

"At this time of the night?" I asked. "Why?"

"I am afraid we cannot say. Just come as quickly as you can," was the reply.

Of course, being a traditional sort of bank, catering for a certain type of client, they summoned me in such a polite way that I almost felt guilty asking. *Have they discovered that money is missing?* I wondered. That was the logical answer, but unlikely. There was no way they were as smart as me. My only decision was: should I do as they asked or make a break for it?

Thirty minutes later, expensively suited and booted, the sartorial epitome of the young and successful city banker, I stepped into the taxi that had been sent for me, and as the black cab raced across town, I considered my options. Deny everything, beg for mercy or... I couldn't think of any others. In the end, I decided to brazen it out. After all, this is what Grandma would have done.

Arriving outside the grey-stone offices, I squared my shoulders and marched through the revolving doors. Crossing the acres of polished-stone foyer with its glittering chandeliers, I fabricated a nonchalance that belied my inner turmoil. Reaching the lift, I paused, took a deep breath and, preparing for the inevitable, stabbed my thumb on the button for the executive suite.

On my way to the thirteenth floor, not the best of omens, I considered whether I might hold any get-out-of-jail-free cards. The answer to that depended not only on what they knew but also whether they wanted to keep any crime as quiet as I did. More importantly, if they were on to me, I needed to know who had dobbed me in.

I could only think of one possibility: Jean, my best friend Bertie's new wife. Had she betrayed me? It was unlikely but possible, I supposed. I had mentioned my plans to her in passing one night when we were lying in bed together. The fact that this particular episode had happened on her hen night when a strategic migraine had forced her to leave early probably meant that she had more to lose than me. I had told no one else, but somewhere along the line it appeared that I had made a mistake and left a trail.

As the lift sped skyward, I struggled to focus, my mind dancing back to my last day at the inner-city comprehensive I sporadically attended. I had been called to the headmaster's office, where – face red with rage, spittle flying from his mouth – he screamed that I was undoubtedly the vilest pupil ever to grace his establishment. Not being born with either the intelligence or the character to make my way in the world, he told me, I was doomed to a life of poverty, petty crime and imprisonment. Then, attitude changing, he had begged me, one more time, to tell him what I knew about the mysterious emptying of the school's bank account. I allowed myself a brief smile. If he thought I was the worst pupil when at least three of my classmates were doing bird for murder, then I must have been a challenge indeed.

While I might not have either intelligence or character, what I did have was a criminal disposition to rival that of my grandma. On my first day at school, I already knew that I wanted to follow in her footsteps and become the world's best confidence trickster. Even then, I knew not to let the slightest hint fall and when asked what I wanted to be when I grew up, I dutifully replied, "A banker, miss."

By ten, I was already helping her with some of her simpler scams and swindles. At seventeen, a fabricated education in an exclusive Swiss boarding school had gained me a place at Cambridge, along with a substantial bursary.

*

As the lift pinged its arrival, my confidence exploded. What did they know, the headmaster and these city types? Their sense of privilege and conceit was astonishing. They really did think that they were better than me. Once I had understood this, their self-satisfied arrogance was easily managed to my advantage. Within days of receiving the bank's offer of employment, I sat at a tiny chipboard desk jammed against the window of my damp and mouldy Brixton bedsit and made my plans. By the time I actually started work, I had already made my first one hundred grand.

"The trick was," said Grandma, "to get started quickly before anyone even knew you were there, let alone believed that you were capable of anything wicked."

Then you stepped away and let the plan mature, slowly, like a fine wine or cheese. No checking how much was being misdirected, no accessing the Belarus account. Just ignore it and let it tick along. It was when you changed your plans, got greedy, or carried out some unexpected activity that they got suspicious and started to investigate.

Exiting the lift, I was met by a very tired and stressed Bertie, one of the bank's more junior auditors. On seeing him, I relaxed a little, my breathing eased, and my mind cleared. If Bertie was involved, there couldn't be anything much for me to worry about and he certainly wouldn't be greeting me if he had been the one to uncover my fraud. Also, he was too insignificant and stupid for anyone to involve him in anything serious.

In that I was wrong.

Stepping into the board room, I saw in front of me the entire main board of the bank and my blood turned to ice. This was big. With little other choice, I took a deep breath and turned on the charm. I became everything that a young successful broker at an exclusive London bank should be. Oozing superciliousness and without waiting to be asked, I took the only remaining seat at the large, impossibly polished oak table, leaving Bertie to stand uncomfortably in the corner. Looking around, I paused, and, after a suitable wait, smiled and asked, "How can I help you gentlemen this bright Sunday morning?"

There followed several seconds of embarrassed silence and shuffling of papers. Eventually, one of the more senior directors cleared his throat and, in a rather embarrassed voice, said, "We have lost fifty million pounds."

"That's a little careless of you," I replied. "How? Where?"

"Over an extended period is all we know. We have no idea how it happened, exactly how much or where it has gone." He continued, "The loss has been over a range of accounts, including a few that you manage."

I held my breath.

"It started before you joined us, so as one of the few people in the clear and, I am told," he hesitated and, clearing his throat again, continued, "one of our brightest rising stars. We need you to investigate."

He looked around as if seeking confirmation. The rest of the board nodded.

"Needless to say, under no circumstances should the police be involved. Do you understand?"

I nodded. I agreed with that last sentiment absolutely.

"Of course," I replied. "I will do everything I can to resolve the situation. I will need a few hours to get my initial thoughts together. Could we meet again later, shall we say midday? Then I'll let you know how I propose to proceed."

Without giving them any chance to respond, I stood up and walked out of the room. *Leave them wondering and don't give them any time to think*, I told myself. I needed to sort a few things, but if all went well, by this evening Bertie would be looking at a long stretch and Jean would be mine.

On my way down in the lift, I was distracted by a buzzing from my mobile – an incoming message. Were they calling me back? Had Bertie confronted Jean after all, and she had confessed to everything? What I read on the screen was, however, much more troubling. It made the hairs on my neck stand to attention. If it was real, the message changed everything. I read it a second time, just to be sure.

Don't be greedy, it read. *The knack is knowing when to take the money and run – Love, Grandma.*

It was not just the content that surprised, more the fact that my grandma had been dead for nearly three years. And I should know, I had watched her plunge to the ground when her parachute had failed to open.

*

The deepest of blue oceans darkened to black as the blazing red sun settled slowly behind the wispy orange-edged clouds. I sipped my oh-so-dry martini and squeezed Jean's hand. The end of another perfect day in paradise.

"Do you think the bank is still trying to figure out where the fifty mill has gone?" she asked.

"I would bet that they are still sitting in that office waiting for me to come back," I answered. "They probably haven't put two and two together, even now."

Leaning over, I kissed her and, as I did, my new burner phone pinged. Reading the message, I felt my joy turn to confusion.

"What's wrong?"

"Nothing really, but it looks like we will have to leave here for a while."

"Why, are they on to us?"

"Nothing like that," I said, showing her the screen.

As she read it, her mouth dropped open and a thrill of anticipation ran through me. It said: *Are you ready for the next adventure? – Love, Grandma. P.S. Bring Jean.*

LIVES OF QUIET DESPERATION

I am looking for a new job. The truth be told, I have been thinking about a change of career for nearly two hundred years now. First, the industrial revolution, with those dark satanic mills belching smoke, soot crusting my clothes and choking my lungs, and now the internet, with its twenty-four-seven demands for my attention. I have nothing left to give.

Of course, finding a new profession at my age is filled with complications. Let's be honest, thousand-year-old mythical beings are not well adapted for work in the cyber age.

"So, what experience of TeethCollect AI do you have?" they ask.

"None actually, but I can deliver presents – many, many presents. Presents to every good girl and boy in the whole world," I explain, "and all in one night."

"Interesting, but what makes you think you are in a position to judge the goodness or otherwise of a minor?" they reply.

And so it goes: "I am afraid that your experience is not

really suited to our current vacancy of Tooth Fairy Class 2. We prefer a more personalised service."

And what could be more personal than delivering to nearly every house in the world? I wonder. Of course, no one ever comes clean on the real reason for my rejection. That I am wingly challenged and rather too plump to purloin discarded teeth from under pillows. That would be discriminatory.

You may not know this, but the only way for a fabled entity such as myself to escape the drudgery of eternity is to die and for that to happen, it is mandatory that no one believes in you anymore. Seriously, can you imagine a situation where all the children in the world, every single one, all stopped believing in Santa at the same time? Impossible, you say. It's just not going to happen, is it? And you would be right. That was the speech I gave myself every year, until…

*

It was a Tuesday early in February. I remember it clearly. I was quality checking a toy bus to ensure that its wheels did indeed go round and round all day long when an idea came to me like a lamp lighting in my head. It was so bad, so downright evil, that I forgot to breathe and had a minion elf not bumped me with a trolly full of seconds, I might be holding my breath even now. My concept, although simple, held within it the real possibility of making every brat in the world abandon me. No one would celebrate Christmas ever again.

My plan required some sacrifices on the part of

others, it is true. For example, the theft of Norway's entire hydroelectricity supply caused nearly half its population to freeze that first winter and those that did survive were forced to move south to much warmer climes. Now, the country is largely deserted, but who cares? Not me. All those pretty, sparkly fjords and those glistening Northern Lights. Ugh.

I did, of course, make some exceptions even for Norway. I saved a small group of Sámi nomads to maintain my supplies of low-speed anthropomorphic propulsion units, or talking reindeer as some elves still insist on calling them. They now live lives of quiet desperation, shivering in the icy wastes of Svalbard, but at least they are still breathing.

These days, my sleigh is powered primarily by nuclear fission. Faster and more reliable than flying mammals it may be, but when you need to land on a snow-covered roof or gain altitude in a tight cul-de-sac, hoof power is difficult to beat. Unfortunately, the speed I now travel is not really compatible with reindeer physiology and so I tend lose a few each year. But hey, there are plenty more fish in the sea, or rather Rudolphs in the tundra. So why should I worry?

But I digress. For my plan to work, I needed to transform some ten thousand hectares of frozen arctic to the cultivation of top-grade skunk. Hence all that power. It was the same with the crystal meth production. Diverting the global supply of cough syrup and replacing it with sugar water was simple enough, but it soon became obvious that people were noticing that their expectorant was no longer cutting the mustard. Even if they could find any on the supermarket shelves. Out of an abundance of caution, I decided to shift blame by diverting attention towards the alt-right network. With a few well-placed Insta posts and the occasional mention of the Illuminati, I soon had the lack of working medicine inextricably linked to a stolen presidential election and, once that happened, I was home free. A few thousand died in the ensuing riots, I admit, but their sacrifice to further my goal was, I feel, a price worth paying.

Of course, I couldn't manage all of this on my own, so after much deliberation, I shared my ideas with a few of my most loyal and specially trained acolytes: the Secret Santa Squad. With them on board, things went swimmingly and in less than two years, I was ready to proceed. So, this Christmas, every kid in the world, regardless of behaviour, will receive, direct from Santa, a special gift of hash brownies and crystal meth mentos. If that doesn't do the trick, nothing will. My moment of destiny had finally arrived.

Waiting for take-off, I allowed my thoughts to wander to Christmases past. At first, this job was much simpler. Receiving a modest wooden elf-made toy satisfied the cravings of even the greediest of children. More and bigger is now the only measure of satisfaction. Also, there is the ever-present threat of parental legal action if, heaven forbid, I do not deliver to order. And as for those namby-pamby, liberal do-gooders telling me that not giving presents to naughty children is an infringement of their human rights, it just makes me weep.

Sluggishly at first, and then gathering pace, my overburdened sleigh battled into the air. Struggling to keep pace, one or two reindeer fell by the wayside: Prancer 348 and Dancer 675, I think. Damn, they were two of my best, but never mind; one must be prepared to suffer losses in the interests of the greater good. That is to say, my future happiness.

Finally airborne, my race against the night began. Taking it easy at first, I visited a few sparsely inhabited Pacific islands to get into the swing of things. My body shook at the thrill of delivering those first gifts. I hadn't felt this alive for at least five hundred years.

Leaving Polynesia behind, I gained speed and headed for New Zealand, my first major population centre. But as I approached the North Island and began to lose altitude, something felt wrong, very wrong indeed. Was I being paranoid? Probably. Surely no one could possibly know what I was up to.

It was then that I saw them, two F16 jets. Dark and menacing, they moved in fast. Being approached by air defences is not as unusual as you might think. Normally, a cheery wave from me has the pilots rubbing their eyes in disbelief and, rather than press the issue, they just peel away and leave me in peace.

Tonight, however, was different. No rubbing, no peeling, just a waggle of the wings and a downward jabbing of thumbs. Not wanting to get on the wrong end of a heat-seeking missile, I obeyed and, gliding ever lower, I switched off my reactor and landed on reindeer power alone.

It was then that everything went wrong. As I came to a gentle halt on the tarmac, I was plunged into darkness as someone pulled my hood down over my eyes. If that wasn't humiliating enough, my attacker then yanked my beard so hard that I lost my balance and fell, hitting the ground with a bone-crushing thump.

"Shit, that hurt," I screamed.

Fortunately, a millennium of only one night's exercise a year has left me with plenty of padding, so no serious damage was done. After a couple of minutes, I had recovered enough to allow me to stagger to my feet. What was happening? In all the time I have been doing this job, no one had ever treated me with such disrespect. Taking a deep breath and swallowing hard, I tore the hood away.

And there, in front of me, was a vision so terrible that even in my worst nightmares I could never have imagined it. At the end of the runway, shining and sparkling in the moonlight, was a second fully-loaded sleigh, reindeer and all. Even worse, it was surrounded by the familiar smirking faces of the Secret Santa Squad. Unemployed and unemployable without me, the little shits had grassed me up to save themselves.

Fists clenched, I wobbled over towards them, but before I even got close, I was ambushed from behind and rugby tackled to the ground. Giving me no chance to get up, the elves grabbed me, four to each limb, and dragged me bodily across the asphalt.

While the attackers on my arms hauled me onto the sleigh, the rest encouraged me to move faster by poking my bottom with sharp sticks and, within minutes, scuffed and sore, I was firmly seated.

Before I had any chance to catch my breath or attempt any sort of escape, a mighty slap on Rudolph 785's derriere made him jump forward and, once more, we were heading skyward.

Tears poured down my cheeks. My last chance of deliverance in ruins, I was going to be delivering bloody presents to uncounted numbers of ungrateful children for the rest of eternity. Burning with a fury to match the red of my tunic, I sought a fitting punishment for the elf betrayal. One option came to mind but was I despicable enough to employ it?

Turning, I watched as the elves, now shrinking in the distance, stared back at me with their blank moronic expressions. That made my decision for me, despicable it was.

At the top of my voice, my breath instantly freezing in the cold night air, I screamed out, "You conniving bunch of bastards, I will get you for this. You are very naughty elves indeed, each and every one of you. None of you will receive a Christmas present ever again. I can do it, you know; I know where you live."

NOW AND THEN

NOW

It's hardly surprising that I nodded off. Her room, roasting under the twin attacks of an overly high thermostat and the feeble winter sun pushing its way through her pathetically thin curtains, was hotter even than the Palm House at Kew.

Her voice, once so commanding but now little more than a whisper, struggled to rouse me and even when it did, it took me a little while to take in what she was saying.

"You bought me roses." For once she was calm. That was unusual these days.

Her words pierced me to the core. Absolutely I had. Only the once, over twenty years ago, the evening we met at the underground station. I went to answer, but she was still talking and, afraid to interrupt in case that thinnest of threads that connected her to the past broke, I kept quiet.

"They were pink. Do you remember? It was the only time you gave me flowers."

Of course I remembered. I thought about that day every time I visited. Meeting her again had given me a second opportunity, and I had blown it. Now, by some miracle, I had been given a third chance.

But this memory, like every other these days, was to her new. While she sometimes recalled flowers, she had never once remembered pink roses. They, or rather it, had been a forced happenstance rather than a deliberate choice, but even so her mind had somehow held onto it.

I looked into her pale eyes, such a light shade of blue that you might have thought them grey, and for the first time in so, so many visits, I saw in them the tiniest sparkle of recognition. My heart leapt.

"I remember everything," I told her, "but the rose wasn't the first time."

There had been, four or five years before that, a daisy. But she had remembered a pink rose and for today, at least, that was good enough for me.

"Tell me. I can't really…"

Her voice trailed off as she struggled to find the words. With no time to lose, I began to speak, desperate to keep her in the here and now, before her light faded once again.

"You were working…" I began, but already I was too late. Her mind, passing briefly through this world, had returned to wherever it lived these days.

THEN

It was a cold, wet January night. Wrapped in my wholly inadequate jacket, I stood outside my local underground station and stewed over what I had just seen and what I should do next. Ignore her, say hello and keep walking; act cool and stop for a quick chat, pretending that nothing bad had happened all those years before, or simply abandon my journey and go home. If the pain of her absence had been bad, then the agony of seeing her again was so much worse.

The last time we had met had been over four years ago, nearly a quarter of my life, but I had recognised her the moment I walked in. Huddled in the far corner of the concourse, she was half-heartedly selling evening newspapers to any interested passer-by. At the sight, my heart skipped, the adrenalin pumped, a cocaine-like rush surged though me and I ran. Had it really been that long since we were together? Of course it had; I had counted every one of those nearly fifteen hundred, mostly sleepless, nights.

My mind went back to the last time, the day after her eighteenth birthday party, the day after… but let's not go there just for the moment. Better to say we had last spoken the day my parents told me we were moving house. With all the maturity that my fifteen years allowed, I knocked on her door and delivered the news. If I was expecting support, a solution, for her to make everything alright, I was misguided. What I got was bitterness, recriminations and an ending. We were no longer boyfriend and girlfriend, our relationship was over. Until the night before, I had never known we were that close, although I had dreamed about it often. Then, slamming the door in my face, that was that. The last time I had seen her, until today.

As the big-flaked snow struggled to escape from its heavy-loaded clouds, I trawled for an answer. As tempting as heading home was, it wouldn't work. I was meant to be meeting friends before going on to a gig and this station had been chosen as the most suitable meeting place. You know the one I mean, logically convenient for everyone but actually handy for no one at all. As this was in the days long before mobile phones, any change to our plans was impossible at this late hour, so I was stuck.

Taking the deepest of breaths, and forcing myself to think, I came up with a plan. At the time, it seemed to make sense. As anyone will tell you, I do not work well under pressure, so the scheme I adopted was, of course, the least workable of all the options available to me.

Right next to me stood a man running a flower stall. "Do you have any red roses?" I asked. "I just want the one."

"No, I do have some pink ones though."

"I guess that will have to do," I answered.

God, I was such a jerk in those days, perhaps I still am. Paying him, I went back inside and, with only the smallest trembling in my knees, I overcame the urge to throw up and walked over to her.

Without raising her eyes, she asked in a bored monotone, "*News* or *Standard*?"

"Neither," I replied. Then she looked up.

"Is that you, boy? My, you're all grown up." Then she saw the flower. "Are you f***ing crazy?"

"Probably," I said, "but it is what it is. When do you finish work?"

"In about thirty minutes."

"How about dinner to make up for me being such a cheapskate that I could only be bothered to buy you a single rose and a pink one at that."

She nodded and gave me the briefest of smiles. It was one of those ones that had always swapped the relative position of my heart and stomach.

"I'll be back in twenty-five."

"Don't be late. I won't wait." That smile again.

I walked out on air, this time the adrenalin bringing me the best high ever, and then reality struck. My friends were due, and there was no way on earth I could let them meet her. They would be sure to ruin everything.

For once in my life, I had been early, the first to arrive. I was still the only one there, so I had time, but not much. What I should do was meet them outside, get them to accept I wouldn't be going with them, passage them through the station and onto a train. All without her seeing me with them, or them her. But how could I manage that?

I prayed for an answer. I knew that I was asking for a miracle on the scale of getting the Red Sea to part, one that was something far beyond that which mere mortals like me are entitled to. But I reckoned I must be owed a divine favour or two, so I asked anyway. Whichever God was on duty that evening smiled at my audacity and took mercy on me.

As my best friend arrived and jumped from the still-moving bus, the answer came to me. Of all of them, he was the most gullible and would surely bite on any fly I cared to cast. Then I would rely on him to convince the others.

"I've got a problem with tonight. I need to go home and sort out a family issue."

He looked surprised, but, wide-eyed, he accepted my deception.

"I only came here to see whether you could sell my ticket for me," I continued. That clinched it. He knew how important this evening was to me. There was no way I would cancel for anything less than a life-or-death situation.

Not naturally curious, he didn't even ask for the details. Had it been any of the others, I don't think I would have got away with it so easily. He just nodded and, tucking the ticket into his altogether more sensible winter coat, he bade me goodbye.

If you know the area, Northolt Station stands on top of a small hill, created no doubt to allow the tracks to pass underneath the road. At the bottom there was, and perhaps still is, a robust wooden bus shelter. My plan consisted of nothing more than to pretend I was catching a bus and then hide until everyone had gone. As long as the right bus didn't actually come along, then everything should be okay.

As I entered, I glanced at my rather battered California dial watch – a twelfth birthday present. Already I only had fifteen minutes left. Could the others not get on with it and arrive?

I had been right about the bus shelter though. Its window gave me a perfect view of the station while, at the same time, concealing me.

Eventually they all turned up, although it was a fine-run thing. With six minutes remaining, the final one arrived and, able to relax, I abandoned my hidey-hole and ran back up the hill. At twenty-seven minutes precisely, their heads disappeared down the escalator. To this day, I have never told any of them the truth about that evening. I now had nothing to do but focus all my attention on the pre-Raphaelite vision of perfection standing in front of me. She was all packed up and ready to go.

NOW

Placing my hand over hers, I softly rubbed her parchment-thin skin. These days, it was so translucent that every vein shone through like a meandering river. Only three years older than me, she might have been twenty. Her body had aged far too fast, marching to the beat of her crumbling mind. The strong beautiful woman I had once known and loved all these years sat silent, hopelessly lost in the byzantine canyons of her mind. I gave her hand only a gentle squeeze as anything beyond the smallest caress caused her to shrink away in pain and terror. She didn't respond.

THEN

"Do you mind going back to my place before we eat?" she asked as we got on the bus. "I'm freezing and I need a bath."

She held out her newsprint-stained, blue-cold hands for me to see and my mood plummeted. There, on the third finger of her left hand, was a thin gold band.

"Oh this," she said as she saw my face. Waving it at me, she continued. "Nothing to worry about. I'll explain everything."

Wrapping both her arms around one of mine, she moved up close and rested her head on my shoulder.

"Tell me what you have been up to," she said.

My sulk lifting a little, I told her about my missing four years. Dropping out of uni to make it as a rock star – not going well. In turn, she told me of marrying in haste when she thought she was pregnant – false alarm – and now repenting at leisure while her husband did three years for armed robbery.

A few minutes later and now hand in hand, we got off the bus. It was the same stop we had used as kids. Surely she didn't still live with her parents, I worried. My mood darkened again, but I was fretting unnecessarily, although it was a close-run thing. She lived just around the corner from them.

Her flat, small and charity-shop furnished but impeccably clean, was bare of any personal items except for a picture of her standing next to a heavily tattooed, shaven-headed man. They were leaning against a large motorcycle. I had met him at her eighteenth and had disliked him on sight. I suspect he had never even noticed me.

In the photo, she was wearing a white dress – rather incongruous, I thought, until I understood that it must have been taken on her wedding day. I was too scared to ask whether I had made the right guess.

While she ran a bath, I was dispatched to the local fish and chip shop and the nearby off-licence to get food and some beer or, better still, wine.

"You might want to pop into the chemist to get anything else you need," she told me. "Especially if you are going to stay. I hope it's still open," she added with a giggle.

I assumed that she meant for me to get more than just toothpaste and, needing no further encouragement, I ran all the way. Her remark about the chemist had me worried and quite rightly. I was only just in time. The chemist had already taken off her white coat and was about to flip the door sign from open to closed, when, mad-eyed and sweating, I pushed my way in. It made the tiny bell attached to the door jangle wildly. She did not seem pleased to see me.

Five minutes later, with all the essentials covered and a furious chemist now able to go home, I collected a bottle of German white wine and two cod and chips. Tucking the food inside my coat to keep it and me as warm as possible, I held the wine at arm's length to achieve the opposite.

All the way back, I fantasised about her luxuriating in that bath, hoping against hope that she would still be in there. I was in luck, and as I walked in, even sweatier than at the chemist's, she called out.

"If you have wine, pour me a glass. The corkscrew's in the kitchen drawer."

It didn't take me long to find there were only two drawers. Of course it was in the second one I opened. What was inside the first was far more interesting, however. Carelessly thrown to the back and poorly covered by a dishcloth, I found the wedding photograph and, on top of it, the ring. I hugged myself.

It had been a long time since I had had a serious girlfriend. Actually, there had never been anyone since her. Okay, let's be honest, I hadn't had a girlfriend other than her. Every time I got close to someone, the memories of that one night always returned and spoiled everything. Tonight, it appeared my dreams were finally coming true.

Despite my best efforts, the wine was warmer than I would have liked. There were no in-shop coolers in those days. Looking inside her fridge, however, I found a tiny freezer compartment and in it a filled ice-cube tray.

Dropping a couple of cubes into a beaker – she had no proper glasses – and pouring the wine over them, I wandered into the bathroom as though it was the most natural thing in the world. Had I thought about it more, I'm sure I would have lost my nerve and hovered uncomfortably outside, waiting for an invitation.

In the minuscule, steam-filled space, she was lying almost submerged. Hair flowing away from her head like some latter-day Ophelia. Her face was almost the only thing not covered by the steaming foamy water. Other, that is, than two pale breasts that floated through the bubbles, daring me to ignore them.

Why I did what I did next, I will never know. It really wasn't me. Fishing out an ice cube and placing it in my mouth, I knelt over her and, holding her breast, caressed a hard, dark nipple with a mixture of tongue and cube.

Sucking in air, she raised her hands and, dripping water, pulled my head to her face and kissed me hard. After what seemed an eternity, she pushed my head back towards her breast and let out a long sigh. Taking the hint, I carried on.

Much, much later, still wet and dripping, we sat in front of her fire eating our fish and chips and finishing the wine. The chips were, by then, cold and soggy and the wine still warm.

What happened that night didn't change me, but what happened the next, and the next and the next, did. For the first time ever, I found the love and stability that I never knew I craved. Whether it was coincidence or confidence I don't know, but at the same time things changed in the band and we started getting more and bigger gigs. While I now had much more money, the downside was that I had to spend time away from her and I begrudged every moment of it. Not that it seemed to matter to her. However long we were apart, whatever time I arrived home, however dirty and smelly I was from spending nights, five to a grotty Transit van, she didn't seem to care. She was always there, always soft, constantly warm and permanently available.

*

In any Eden, there must be a forbidden fruit, and in that fruit, always a worm. In our case, the fruit was that wedding ring, never discussed, and the worm, the giver of said ring. It was almost six months to the day after our meeting that the worm reared its ugly, and I mean ugly, head.

Arriving home from the recording studio – yes, things were really looking up – with a bottle of good red, I found her in tears, holding the wedding photo.

"They are letting him out early, as long as he has somewhere to go."

"You mean here?"

She nodded.

"Can't you tell them he isn't welcome?"

"I can't do that. I owe him. It's not his fault that there has always been someone else."

Did she mean me? I didn't ask; it didn't matter. I had grown used to being loved and loving and whatever she said now wasn't going to be good enough. I had thought we were forever, but in reality I was only ever a temporary replacement.

If I had had any pride, I would have packed and walked away. Only, I hadn't and didn't. I left, tears running down my cheeks with only the clothes I was wearing. Apparently, I had only ever been a fill-in for motorcycle man and now that he was coming home, I was surplus to requirements.

"Just give me some time. I will sort it out. I promise," were the last sobbed words I heard as I ran down the stairs.

NOW

To simplify things, I was going to tell you that I never heard from her again; well, not until that day when her son – my son, perhaps? No, the timing didn't work – emailed me. But that isn't true. My mother and her kept in touch, a secret that my mother took to her grave. I only discovered this at the funeral when I saw her standing outside talking to the priest. I turned around and drove away, an act for which my brother and sister have never forgiven me. I also saw her once more, much later, in Marks and Spencer, but more of that in a while.

At the end of the email was a phone number, which, after two sleepless nights, I rang. The voice that answered was deep, rough and obviously male, but underneath was an inflection that was unmistakably hers.

"Hello, it's Richard. I got your email."

Over the next few minutes, he explained the problem that she was in a home.

"She wanders," he told me.

"I'm not sure I understand. She escapes from the home?"

"No, her mind wanders. She tells such stories. I am never sure whether they are real or who knows..." His voice drifted away. "The thing is, regardless of where she wanders, she always comes back to the same place."

"And where is that?"

"Not where, who."

"Me?"

He said nothing, but I thought I heard a catch in his breath at the other end of the line.

*

I watched as she slept. For once, she seemed to be at peace. I always felt better when she was like this.

Perhaps I should have stayed, helping her to resolve the situation with motorcycle man. Would things have been any better had I done so? Probably not. Quite likely me being around would have made the whole situation much worse. The fights and later the beatings would still have gone on.

Could I have held and comforted her through the horror of finding him hanging in the communal staircase the day after she told him she was leaving? I don't think so. How could any relationship survive such a trauma? But as usual, I am only thinking of myself. What I really mean is that I couldn't have coped and, selfish man that I am, I left her to face him alone.

Whether it was at this point that her mind started to retreat into itself, I don't know. But I suspect suppressing that terrible sight might have had something to do with it. Fortunately, for both of us, her memories of the incident and indeed him are especially faint, and she rarely remembers. Today, of all days, she chose to. That is, if choice had anything to do with it.

"I never loved him, you know. I told him that I did, but it was a lie. He was exciting and you were too young to help me escape."

Escape from what? I wondered. But it was too late to ask. Even if she could remember, it would only cause distress. Never had she been this open. Why hadn't I had the strength to stay?

"Who do you love?" I asked, not sure whether I wanted to hear the answer.

"My boy and you, of course. Never told you, did I, but it was always you from that first kiss. I was so stupid."

"No, not at all. Just being human."

But what I thought was *why couldn't you have told me that when I was thirteen?* I would have waited my entire life for you. It was not true, of course; in the end, I hadn't waited long at all. The thought of a life alone was too terrifying, so, in the end, I settled for second best.

"I'm so sorry," I said, "it was cruel of me to just walk out."

*

This room was far too warm, stale even. It must be a breeding ground for all sorts of germs and now it was taking control. I found my eyes drifting closed again. I don't know how long I stayed like that, but, at some point, I felt her shift in her chair and, in a voice so distant, it felt on the edge of eternity itself, she told me.

"You were right; it wasn't the first time. How could I have forgotten the daisy? I seem to forget so many things these days."

THEN

So how did we first meet and what happened between us that, even after four years, I was almost unable to face her? More importantly, what has it got to do with a daisy?

I must have been twelve. My mixed family, parents recently remarried, had moved into a council house in a large estate on the western edge of London. I guess, these days, you would call it social housing on a sink estate. However, to the almost teen me, it didn't seem like that at all, and it soon became the haven where I did my growing. All these years later, I still remember it fondly, but that may be more to do with her than anything else.

Every house and flat had two, three, four or more children and all of us were pretty much left to roam the streets or the rough grassland that surrounded three sides of the estate at will. Without any real supervision, we naturally divided into largely self-managing groups; gangs would be too strong a description. Within each group, the elders made the rules, marshalled their troops and – I didn't understand this until much later – protected the youngsters.

I, of course, being the new kid on the block, was an outsider. Sitting on the low brick wall that divided our miniscule front garden from the street, I watched, lonely and unhappy, as the others played under the protective gaze of their leaders. One tribe in particular caught my eye or, more truthfully, it was their chief, a raggedy-haired, cigarette-smoking tomboy of about fifteen, her initials carved onto the inside of her forearm in a homemade tattoo. I was smitten. Silently watching her every move, I hoped for some sort of recognition. If she noticed me at all, she gave no sign, until one memorable day when, as she led her followers into the nearby fields, she turned to me and asked, "Are you coming with us or not, boy?"

I needed no second invitation, although I am sure that there would have been none. I followed on like some faithful Labrador puppy, and soon became a regular, if inconsequential, part of the pack. If she noticed me on any of our later expeditions, she didn't show it and rarely spoke to me directly. For nearly twelve months, I remained at the fringes; ignored at worst, tolerated at best.

It was on my thirteenth birthday, a hot summer's day, that everything changed. We had spent the afternoon negotiating a peace treaty with a rival gang from the estate on the other side of the fields. Under a barrage of obscenities, threats and seduction, the poor boy leading their side had surrendered his position to each and every one of her unreasonable demands.

As we made our way home, the evening still warm and fragrant with freshly mown grass, we lauded her success. She, on the other hand, appeared distracted, eventually sending us all homeward without her. As I passed, she held me back.

"It's your birthday, boy."

I nodded.

"Have you ever kissed a girl?"

My face exploded. Feet shuffling, eyes seeking refuge in the ground, I shook my head.

"Here," she said, turning her cheek in my direction.

I gave it a quick peck.

"If you ever tell anyone I let you do that, you're dead."

Walking on air, I had no reason at all to doubt the truth behind her threat.

After that she seemed to find more and more reasons to be alone with me. All by chance, you understand. Exactly a year later, the others having left, we were contesting who could swing highest on an old tyre strung from a branch. Her, of course.

She turned to me. "Want to kiss me on the lips?"

I had spent most of my waking hours and all my sleeping ones since that first occasion thinking of little else. At least this time I didn't turn red and, full of unwarranted confidence, I walked over to her and planted my lips on hers.

She destroyed me instantly. "That's not how you do it. You need to use your tongue. It's called a Frenchie."

I died inside. I had blown my only chance; the opportunity would never come again. I was mistaken. Demonstrating a surprising and until now unimagined gentleness, she took mercy on me and, pushing her tongue inside my mouth, she moved it between my lips and teeth. Better still, she let me practise until I had a fair idea of what was required. On the way home, I picked her a daisy. She dismissed the gesture with a groan, rolling her eyes heavenward. She did, I noticed with joy, undo a button on her blouse and tuck the tiny white-and-yellow bloom though the newly empty buttonhole.

It would be an exaggeration to say we became boyfriend and girlfriend, or so I thought, but we became close if nothing else. The timing was perfect as it came at the moment she began to change and had there not been a link, I am sure we would have drifted apart. She grew her hair and began to brush it, started wearing dresses that exhibited hitherto unimaginably shapely legs, and, I noticed, was increasingly visited by boys – or, should I say, young men. But in one respect, things remained the same. If I saw her walking towards the fields on her own, I knew that if I followed, I would be rewarded with a Frenchie, and on just one occasion, something a little more.

*

It crept up on me, but suddenly she was eighteen and having a coming-of-age party. Best of all, I was invited. I arrived full of expectation and trailing clouds of unnecessary aftershave. She blanked me.

By far the youngest there, I drifted through the crowds of long-haired, loud almost-men and impossibly beautiful girls, more lost than I had ever been before. I couldn't keep my eyes away from her as – hair woven with flowers; her buttoned dress almost see-through – she danced with a string of older boys. I longed to be close to her, to feel her body against mine, but never got the chance.

Into the room strolled the shaven-headed, motorcycle-riding moron I had seen before. Taking control and placing his arms around her, they slowly circled the darkened living room, her head resting on his shoulder. I could do nothing but watch, until, in shame and misery, I retreated to the garden, taking with me an old and unplayable guitar that lived in the corner of her living room. Hiding myself behind a tree, I strummed at it in a forlorn attempt to play a tune.

"I've been looking for you. I thought you might have gone."

"No, I wanted to, but I was too embarrassed to go without saying goodbye."

"I'm glad."

"Where's motorcycle man?"

"He's gone, thank God. He really is a moron. I just couldn't get away from him."

She reached out her arms and pulled me up. Standing close in the warm night air, the electricity built until, finally, she placed her arms around my neck and, standing on her tiptoes, kissed me. It was soft and slow, and her lips tasted of cigarettes and cheap wine. For the first time ever, it wasn't rushed, and with all fears of discovery gone, we just stood there for everyone to see. Eventually, she pulled away.

"Let's go somewhere quiet."

Lacing her fingers in mine, she led me inside and upstairs. Her home had three bedrooms. From the groans and cries leaking from two of them, it was obvious that they were already in use. The third, hers I guessed, was locked. Reaching up and taking a key from above the frame, she unlocked the door.

"Come inside and close the door," she told me.

Her room, dark and so filled with stale smoke that I could hardly see or breathe, was tiny. Although it was full of teenage detritus, there was only one significant item of furniture: a single bed that was covered with a blanket decorated with cartoon animals. Unlike me, she had inhabited this same space for most of her life.

Squeezing around the bed, she opened the curtains. It allowed me to catch brief glimpses of her lit in the headlamps of the occasional passing car. I went to follow.

"Stay there."

I did as I was told.

Taking all the time in the world, she unbuttoned her dress and let it slip to the floor, the fabric making an almost noiseless rustle as it slid across her skin. Underneath, she was naked; her small breasts and long, long legs topped by a blonde triangle were perfect.

Coming close and kissing me hard, she slipped her hand inside my jeans and I panicked. *She was so much more experienced than me and would laugh at my size. Motorcycle man will be so much bigger and obviously more practised*, my mind added helpfully. At these thoughts, I wilted.

She must have read my mind.

"Don't worry, boy. Everything will be perfect."

Covering my face and neck with a thousand small kisses, she unbuttoned and removed my jeans, followed by my underpants. Stroking me until I was hard again, she rolled a condom onto me. She did it so gently that I could hardly feel her touch.

Falling back on the bed, she pulled me on top of her and, legs wide, helped me inside. She was already wet. As I entered her, she let out a kittenish mewing cry and, with one hand holding my neck tight, gave me the deepest, longest Frenchie ever. Her other hand gripped my behind and, pushing down, she set the rhythm. Knowing no better, and desperate to impress, I counted the thrusts. As I got to five, she lifted her hips and, tightening around me, let out a gasp. That sound echoes in my dreams even today. Overwhelmed, I came. The whole experience had lasted less than two minutes.

Much later, I realised that it was the first time for her as well. But at fifteen and only focused on not making a complete fool of myself, I never thought to reassure her or tell her I loved her. By the time I appreciated how selfish I had been, it was, of course, way too late to do anything about it.

NOW

She was back and talking sense. "Do you remember our first time?"

"I'll never forget. You were my first."

"I can't really remember much about it. Was it any good?"

I almost told her the truth, but that would have been cruel.

What I said was, "It has never been as good with anyone since. I wish it had only ever been you," and I meant it.

I worried that she was going to remember the next day and I didn't want to go there, but instead she took a surprising turn.

"You really were too young; I needed someone who could save me, and I didn't know how to wait for you to grow up. I'm so sorry."

I was elated; somewhere deep within her she still remembered that night and if she remembered it differently to me, protecting herself against what came later, so what? But interestingly, she had apologised for what came next. I had never heard her ask for forgiveness from anyone for anything. My eyes prickled. She had nothing to be sorry for.

"Do you remember what happened next?" I asked.

I was on dangerous ground but needed to know. But I was too late; she had left again.

At first, it was easier to blame her, it took some of the

pain away, but in the end, there was no one other than me at fault. As I said, in every Eden, there is a forbidden fruit, something that can never be discussed, something best left unsaid. In my case, it was my parents or, more precisely, their moving and later motorcycle man. Telling her my news so soon after that night was obviously not the best thing to have done. The selfish part of me was relieved that my parents hadn't told me earlier. Could I have kept quiet, only casually mentioning it, as we lay cuddling afterwards? Probably not. I'm also sure that letting her know beforehand would not have been a good idea.

THEN

I spent the few weeks between the party and moving away avoiding her. I did occasionally go to the swing in the hope that, by some miracle, she had noticed and followed me. She never came.

The night before we finally moved was hot and sticky, and the window to my bedroom was open. At about midnight, lying sleepless, I heard deep and animalistic sounds coming from the direction of the swing. Louder and louder, higher and higher until it climaxed with a groan and an exclamation. Fascinated and at the same time repelled, I buried my head in my pillow, but it did no good. I had no need to wonder who the pair were. I might have been her first, but now she had given herself to him and I had lost her forever.

NOW

"Are you my husband?"
"No, just a friend."

"Do I have a husband? I don't have a ring."

"He died many years ago, I am afraid." For a second, I thought she would remember, but if she did, it quickly passed.

"You are married, aren't you?" She had never remembered that before. I had told her about my family on my first visit nearly two years ago.

"Not when we knew each other. I got married later, much, much later, after we stopped seeing each other. I am divorced, but I have a son and a daughter."

"Do they know you come to see me?"

"Yes, they do."

"Do I have children?"

"Yes, of course, you have a son. He is the spitting image of his dad." Shit. Why had I said that? I prepared for tears again, but she seemed to miss it.

"Why doesn't he visit me?"

"He does; he visits you every Saturday and I come to see you on Sundays."

"If you have a family, why are you here with me?" A good question.

'Because I love you', I wanted to say, but all I said was, "It's complicated."

That seemed to satisfy her and, the light fading from her eyes, her lids flickered and closed. I wanted her to keep talking, but I let her rest.

Why was I here? A good question, as I said. Initially, because her son had emailed me out of the blue. How he had obtained my address, I never found out. As I said, he told me that his mum was in a care home with something called vascular dementia, a horrifying disease that delivers hundreds of mini strokes each day. Every one of them steals a tiny memory that will never return. In her distress, he told me, she kept asking for me.

It was a difficult conversation with my ex-wife. I guess I didn't need to tell her, but I felt she should know. Whether I needed to tell her everything, I'm not sure, but anyway that's what I did and, after the tears and recriminations, she told me that visiting was the right thing to do. So, each Sunday I drive up from Sussex and spend the afternoon with her. Sometimes, like today, we reminisce, other times I read to her, and most frequently we just sit, each lost in our own world.

THEN

I could have gone back to her, perhaps I should have. Instead, being a coward, I stayed away, although I sought her out in every crowded shop, every city street, hoping and praying that she would be there. Sometimes I would catch a glimpse of someone almost but not quite her. And each time I did, a little bit of me died. Then, one day, I settled for second best and married someone else. Even then, to my shame, I kept watch with half an eye. As you might imagine, my marriage was not a success.

It must have been ten years after I married. Recently divorced, I was in London with my ex-wife and kids, buying them shoes, I think. And there she was. This time, it really was her. On the downward escalator, she passed me as I was travelling up, giving out a false picture of a happy family. As she passed, she smiled and mouthed hello and I almost jumped the barrier. The craving to be with her had not waned, but, somehow, I resisted. As I reached the top, my resolve wavered and I turned around, ready to go down and join her. But I hesitated and as I watched, now on solid ground, she walked through the doors and out of my life. She did not look back.

"Who was that?" asked the ex-wife.

"Someone I knew as a kid." Even then, I couldn't admit the truth, that there had never been anyone other than her. Not even the mother of my children.

"Pretty," she said.

Pretty. I almost exploded, you have no idea. But I kept quiet, and that was it. We never spoke of her again, until that email arrived.

NOW

They say that the teenage heart is quick to repair. That was not my experience, but the adult heart, as I now know, never heals.

I must have dozed again, dreaming of my past, until the harsh clang of the bell marking the end of visiting time brought me back to reality. Reaching out for her, I pulled back. Her hand was cold and still. I opened my eyes. Her head slumped to one side and her open, unblinking eyes told me she had gone. She was smiling though.

I should have called for help, but what good would that have done? The nurses would come soon enough to chivvy me along. I would wait until they did; after all, this was going to be my last visit.

Had I done any good coming all this way every week? Did these Sundays make any difference to her? If you had asked me only a week ago, I would have said probably not. But after today, who knew?

I leant across and gently kissed her on the forehead.

"I love you," I told her. "There has never been anyone other than you." And as my tears fell, I wondered why I had never said that before. If only I had been sufficiently brave that first night or when we re-met, then things might have been so different. It was too late now, so with little else to do until someone came along, I sat back in my chair, closed my eyes and, holding her hand, remembered those small parts of our lives we had shared.

THE MALLORCAN JOB

The answer had not come to Ken fully formed; he told me that first evening as we drank ice-cold beer and watched the immense orange sun set over the headland. It had arrived gradually, taking the ten or more years between his first trip to the island – when the little problem, as he called it, first occurred – and now. A whisper here, a murmur there during the quiet moments of the day and an occasional hint in his dreams. And then, one morning, there it was. The first I knew about any of this was when, excited at finally having a solution, he had sent a message to the entire group chat, including me. That had been a mistake, I later discovered.

I think I have solved our little problem. If nothing else, it gives us an excuse to go back to Mallorca. We need to meet up soon and work out the details.

Sounds good, I replied, *but I have no idea what you are talking about.*
Sorry! That message wasn't meant for you, came the

reply, *but as you now know, why not come along anyway? You always seem to enjoy yourself when you are there.*

I wish I could afford it, but money is tight at the moment, I replied.

Messaging complete, I let my mind wander back to the day I first met Ken and the others. I was eleven and it was our first day at our new school. We spent the next few years together, growing up, but, on reflection, growing older might be a better description.

Later, a mixture of carelessness, family and work on my part caused me to lose contact. We might have been together for seven years, but the break lasted over thirty and by the time we met again, my memories of school were so faded that I could hardly separate one person or event from the next.

So when, like a bolt from the blue, an email arrived in my junk folder from someone called Terry, I struggled to put a face to the name. I was tempted to discard it along with the many others offering Eastern European brides and millions to be paid into my account. However, a nagging at the back of my mind prompted me to open it.

Do you want to come to a barbeque at Paul's? the mail asked.

Work was winding down by then and I was no longer spending months and years in the more dubious parts of the world. It seemed like a good time to reconnect.

I remember the day well. I could hardly forget; it changed my life. Bright and sunny it might have been, but from the moment I arrived, I was uncomfortable. Everyone other than me had stayed in touch. With their stories and lingo, they might have belonged to some secret society that I was not party to. I felt completely alone. Regardless, I did my best to join in, and as everyone appeared pleased to see me, I said yes to joining another get-together later that year. This rather riotous party was followed by another, and yet another, until I was a regular attendee at, as I thought, all their reunions. Little did I know that I was being assessed for my suitability to join what actually was a secret society.

Don't get me wrong, these were not frequent gatherings. Just meeting up in a local pub or someone's home a few times a year. At one of these, someone, it might have been Terry, suggested that we could take a short holiday to Mallorca. Everyone other than me had been there the year previously, when, apparently, the little problem had occurred.

"We could have a look around for old time's sake, to see whether we can solve it," he explained.

Everyone, including me, bought into the idea and the next March we spent five days in the sun, eating, drinking and reminiscing. To help us along, Terry tested our memories with quizzes on school, our hometown and the music of our youth.

The trip was so successful that we all signed up to go again the next year, and the year after, and then again, the year after that. Actually, we went every year for the next six years. I never noticed anyone addressing the little problem, not in my hearing anyway. We would have probably carried on in this manner until we had to be lifted from the plane, had the pandemic not got in the way and we were forced to cancel.

Two years later, Covid defeated and travel opened

up again, we all fully intended to take the trip we had promised ourselves. Unfortunately, by then, hyperinflation and the subsequent collapse of sterling brought about by the Russia-Ukraine War made foreign holidays, for me at least, a distant dream. It was in the middle of this reverie that a ping from my mobile brought me back to the real world. It was Ken again.

No need to worry about the cost. If my plan works out, we'll be going for nothing.

There followed a flurry of exchanges. Everyone liked the idea but arranging a date to meet up and plan didn't prove to be that easy. *How on earth could a bunch of sixty-somethings be that busy?* I wondered. But what with socialising, grandchildren and hospital appointments, it ended up being nearly three months before we were able to get together. The venue: another barbeque at Paul's. Had I known that behind all this bonhomie the others were making plans for my future, I might not have anticipated the event with so much enthusiasm.

*

In early October, the weather squally and cold, it was not really the right day to spend time in the garden, but Ken insisted.

"Let's go for a walk," he said. Ken spoke as he always did, soft and low and from the corner of his mouth.

"This afternoon," he told me. "You are going to hear some things that we have kept secret from you and almost everyone else in the world for a long time. Over forty years, in fact."

"Hold on a second," I said, struggling to hear what he was saying, "let me get on your other side so my good ear is closest to you."

As I moved around, he carried on talking.

"Can you repeat what you just said?" I asked. "I didn't catch it."

Ken sighed and raised his voice. "I said: This afternoon, you are going to hear some things that we have kept secret from you and everyone else for a long time, over forty years. You are the only one here who doesn't know, and we think it is time you were brought in on the secret."

"What secret? What are you talking about?" I asked.

"How can I put this? Perhaps we have not been completely straight about what we do for a living."

"What! Surely you are an engineer, Paul an accountant and Terry a schoolteacher?"

He laughed. "Well, no, but that is what we tell people."

"Have you been lying to me all this time?"

"Yes, but I don't think you have much to complain about, do you? You've not been completely straight with us either."

My blood ran cold. How had he found out? Something told me that it wasn't worth trying to deny the truth, so instead I asked, "How long have you known?"

"Since just before that first barbeque," Ken replied. "We were doing some research when we came across your name. At the time, we thought that you might be useful to us. That was why we asked you along. Since then, we have been discussing whether we could trust you. To be completely straight, we need to go back to Mallorca to complete some unfinished business from before your time − a stain on our reputation, if you will. Knowing what your real job is, we decided to ask for your help. You are very good, I'll say that. We have been testing you every time we meet and never once have you let your cover slip. In fact, it was so perfect that many of us thought that our information might be wrong, and that you really did work for that computer company."

My shoulders sagged. My ex-wife had never suspected; my kids had never found out. Even Jane didn't know, but apparently everyone here did.

"Come back inside, and let's have a little chat." And with that, he walked into the conservatory, a slight limp in his right leg. Arthritis, he had always told me. A fall from a high roof, as I was to discover only a few minutes later.

I followed him inside to find that all the chairs except one had been drawn into a rough semicircle and everyone else was already seated. The final chair – empty, a straight-backed, hard-seated kitchen model – had been placed facing the others. With no other choice, I dropped onto it and faced the inquisition.

"We," said Terry, once I had made myself as comfortable as I could, "have been working together, pretty much since school, providing certain premium and difficult-to-obtain services to high-wealth individuals across the globe. Each of us has certain specialised skills to enable us to be a one-stop shop for meeting our clients' needs. Because people in their position value discretion above all things, our approach appeals and has been the foundation for our success. It reduces the risk of discovery and, in some cases, capture, you see. Let me introduce you to the truth about your friends.

"Paul is the world's foremost expert in money laundering. Most operations can only clear about ten pence in the pound. He can normally achieve eighty to ninety pence, less our fifteen per cent, of course."

I looked at him in a new light. "And Christina knows all about this?" I asked.

He laughed. "Of course." He turned towards his wife. "You explain your role, dear."

"It's simple," she replied, laughing. Leaning back in her chair, she stretched her arms wide. "As our chief salesperson, I keep the whole ship afloat. When things get a bit slack, I fly around the world and drum up sufficient new business to keep everyone occupied."

My mind was in a whirl. This was crazy. "And the rest of you?"

Terry looked around and, once everyone had nodded, reintroduced them to me, starting from the left.

"John is our creative accountant. One of his main tasks for the last twenty years or so has been to manage the personal accounts of a certain powerful US family. He stopped in 2016 when we started to realise that there were limits to how much even John's genius could hide. Karen looks after the logistics of moving people and things around the globe."

Terry passed him and Sue by and carried on with Maureen. "Mo is responsible for finding suitable wheels when we need them, and Trev is our hacker. He has worked with major airline reservation systems for years. This has given him a legitimate reason to access databases as a cover to obtain building and alarm system plans. He also changes government, airline and hotel records to show that we have never been where our work takes us. Linda is the organisational brains behind our work and Ken is our master cat burglar and cracksman."

"So how did you find out about me?" I asked.

"We had a commission," Ken answered, "reuniting the Russian Imperial Crown Jewels with the Romanov family. You might not have heard about it as the Russians did their best to bury the news."

"I did hear rumours," I answered.

"Well, anyway, I had got inside the Hermitage Museum in St Petersburg, liberated the merchandise, and was on my way down when I slipped and fell. I broke my leg in three places. Hence the limp."

Karen continued, "We had to get Ken out of the country fast, but we needed some support. We, or rather Trevor, hacked into the British Embassy system in Moscow to find the names of some expats who might be able to help. That was when we came across your name in a certain very well-hidden folder."

"But you never came to me," I stuttered.

"No, we might be criminals, but we are also your friends," she replied. "We would have only put you at risk as a last resort. Anyway, we found a financier who didn't want certain photographs released to the world. He drove Ken to Finland for us."

"But we haven't covered everyone," I said. "What about you other three?"

"Sue and I," replied Terry, "run what might be described as our charitable foundation. If someone needs a new start in life, perhaps a deposed dictator or a financier whose hands have been caught in the till, Karen and Linda deliver them to our place in France. There, Sue builds a new identity for them, while I create all the necessary documents. Trev helps, of course, by updating the relevant computer systems, suitably backdated with their new identity."

"And that just leaves Ian," I said. Ian was sitting a little apart from the rest. His eyes were cold as they stared at me and in the softest of voices, one so quiet that I had to lean forward to hear, he simply said, "I eliminate any difficulties that might jeopardise our success." He smiled at me, but only with his mouth.

"And so," said Terry, "that's everyone. Now we need to discuss the problem at hand. Do you remember the first time we went to Mallorca?"

I nodded.

"Before then, we had completed a contract there. Unfortunately, it all went a bit Pete Tong and security became so tight that we were unable to transfer the goods to our client. The difficulty of doing such a large job on a small island, I suppose. Each time we have gone back, we have checked that the cargo is still well hidden and tried to figure out a way of getting it to our clients. Finally, as you know from the WhatsApp, Ken thinks he has come up with an answer. We all believe that it can work, but we need your help. If we are successful, your share will be one mill, all expenses paid. Tax-free of course," he added, almost as an afterthought. "More than enough to cover the easyJet flight. Is that acceptable to you?"

"I guess so, but what are these goods you are talking about?"

"Palma Cathedral, as you may know," replied Terry,

"has, or rather had, a rather unique medieval stained-glass window. It went missing. It was all over the news, if you remember. The job was quite a success really. No one has ever managed to explain how nearly two tons of priceless glass could be removed from high up on the eastern end of the nave in a single night without anyone noticing."

I had to be honest, I was impressed. These people – I was not sure whether I now knew them well enough to call them my friends – were good. I was certainly prepared to consider doing what they asked.

Since Trev's retirement, I was told, his capacity to hack into networks had been somewhat diminished. Obviously, the group didn't want to use their own passports, as Terry, who it was becoming clear was the leader, was uncomfortable with the idea. It made the risks unnecessarily high. What was needed, he had decided, were real documents and this was where I came in. As they had discovered, my job for the few months leading up to my retirement had been doing exactly that. I liaised with the passport office to obtain the real thing for employees of certain government agencies. For a cool million, what they expected from me was easy-peasy. All I had to do was approach my contacts, provide them with some up-to-date photos and the details I wanted printed on the documents and voilà. By return, I would receive twelve genuine UK passports issued from a certain numbered series, which ensured that they were difficult to cancel and would avoid any checks at border control.

As I was about to retire, how could I be sure that I would get away with such a thing, you may wonder. It was simple: I knew how the system worked. As people were often asked to do odd jobs after they left the service, no one actually got around to revoking anyone's security clearance until at least six months after they had gone. To be doubly sure, I let all my contacts know that I would probably be back to submit the occasional request, so no questions would be asked. Of course, someone would eventually get around to checking what I had been up to, but the backlog of work was so great that it would be at least a year, if ever. We had plenty of time.

*

Nearly six months later, early March, the 737 bumped onto the runway in Palma. And there, amongst the crowds, indistinguishable from the hundred or so other passengers on board, were twelve typical elderly tourists, looking forward to their holiday in the sun. If any of the group was suffering from nerves, they certainly weren't showing it. As my part was already over, there was, strictly speaking, no need for me to be there, but I wanted to tag along for the craic. So, there I was on that first evening, standing with Ken on the hotel terrace, enjoying the dying sun and a beer.

Our time in Mallorca passed quickly and if there was any planning or activity on the part of the others, it escaped me. We met for breakfast; a light three-course meal comprising fruit, cereal and a full English, followed by an optional continental, then we would walk along the seafront, stopping off to argue whether that had been a porpoise we had seen or to wait for Christina to finish her paddle. Most days, we had coffee or beer at a seafront café run by a short dark-haired local who everyone seemed to know. Drinks finished, we ambled back to the hotel just in time to sample a pre-lunch sangria at the poolside bar before partaking of another three-course meal. Except for Wednesday, when we held the quiz, people did their own thing in the afternoons. Normally I went into town to do some shopping or walked to the deserted nature reserve at the end of the bay in a vain attempt to walk off all that food. Occasionally, I ran into some of the others doing the same thing.

At six prompt, we met in the bar to have drinks before yet another full meal. Struggling to our feet, we moved back to the bar or, if warm, the terrace, where we spent the rest of the evening regaling each other with the same stories that we had told on every previous visit. It was the same procedure this year as every year.

On the last evening, as I was slipping into my chair and preparing to order a long cool drink, Ken approached me.

"Do you want to watch it all going down?" he asked. "It will involve missing dinner."

I nodded. Leading me outside, we got inside a clapped-out Fiat 500, driven by the man who ran the coffee shop. Ken introduced him as Costas.

"An old friend," he explained.

While Costas drove us out of town, Ken described his plan and by the time we stopped at a spot overlooking a dry valley up in the Mallorcan hills, work to recover the window was already underway.

Tiny figures were placing small boxes against some metal doors that blocked the entrance to what appeared to be an old railway tunnel. The boxes in place, the figures retreated behind three old-style Mini Coopers, painted red, white and blue.

"Mo's idea of a joke," Ken told me. "She does tend to overdo the drama at times. A Land Cruiser or F150 would have been a much better bet, but it is what it is."

"Where on earth did she manage to uncover three old wrecks like those on an island?" I asked.

Ken shrugged. "No idea. Don't care."

His last remark was obscured by a loud explosion coming from the boxes. As the smoke and dust cleared, I could see the doors hanging from their hinges. Unfortunately, the blast had also dislodged some large boulders, which now replaced the doors in blocking the entrance.

"For Christ's sake, I only asked them to blow the bloody doors off," he misquoted.

As I watched, the figures cautiously approached and began moving the boulders. That job complete, they went into the tunnel, returning within minutes carrying heavy flat boxes. Loading them into the Minis, they went back to fetch yet more. Collection complete, the Minis drove away in opposite directions, suspension bottoming out on the rough tracks. The weight of the glass, I assumed.

After the cars had disappeared, Ken wandered off, taking Costas with him. While the pair held a whispered conversation in voices too low for me to hear, I took my chance. Pulling out my mobile, I tapped out a short text message, returning it to my pocket as soon as I had finished. I did not wait for a reply. Turning, I saw both Ken and Costas staring at me.

"What next?" I asked, doing my best to keep my voice light.

"Let's go and see how the other end pans out, shall we?" muttered Ken.

We took a long slow drive back towards the hotel, but instead of stopping outside, Costas stayed on the seafront until we reached the end of the bay. Switching off the engine, we waited. After about ten minutes, the first Mini, gunning its engine, passed us by. Within seconds, the other two followed, chased at some distance by an ancient police Seat, sirens blaring and lights blazing.

Without warning, the Minis hit a hard left and, crossing the pavement, drove along the rough sand-and-rock beach towards the nature reserve. The police car saw the change in direction much too late and before they had a chance to follow, two figures stepped out of the shadows and placed a stinger in front of their wheels. In a vain attempt to avoid it, the officers only succeeded in hitting a tree. Steam pouring from its now-buckled front, the Seat stopped dead, leaving its two occupants to watch in frustration as the Minis shrank into the distance.

Waiting for them was a small fishing boat and, a short way offshore, lights extinguished, I thought I saw another much larger boat.

While the cargo was unloaded, the drivers waited in the cars, but as the last box was put on the fishing boat, spotlights blazed from the other boat – a military cutter. Over a megaphone, orders were barked and the fishermen held their hands aloft. However, in the general confusion, the Minis escaped, before being driven back to the road and, I assumed, quietly abandoned in some out of the way place. The local fishermen were left to face the music.

Ken nodded to Costas, who, starting the engine, took

us on a long diversion back to the hotel, avoiding the seafront to remain above suspicion, I guess. No one spoke, but in the front seat, Ken hummed himself a little tune of satisfaction. He didn't seem at all troubled by the setback.

*

If I had expected the others to be disheartened when we got back to the hotel, I was mistaken. We were met by a party in full swing.

"We suspected," explained a rather drunk Trev, "that the authorities would know what we were up to, so we rented an isolated holiday cottage that backs onto a hidden cove, some fifteen miles from here. We moved the glass from a different spot the afternoon we arrived. The whole exercise today was a charade to throw the police off the scent.

"While you watched the Minis being loaded with boxes of broken brick, the real thing was already in a speedboat on its way to Sardinia. It arrived in Italian waters about ten minutes ago."

Our celebration went on long into the night and it was with a very sore head and malevolent pixies stabbing the inside of my eyelids with sharp sticks that I staggered down to breakfast the next morning. I was the only one there. I wasn't surprised. If I was struggling to face any food, how could anyone else? Instead of eating, I wandered outside, which was not a good idea. The brutal Mallorcan sun drilling into my eyes, I was forced to screw them up to see anything at all. So, when my phone rang, it took me a while before I could see who was calling. It was Ken.

"Where are you all?" I asked.

"Most of us are already back in the UK. We checked out shortly after you went to bed last night and caught a late flight home. We didn't want to run the risk of you squealing any more than you already had."

In my delicate state, my mind refused to work fast enough to even think of denying it, so instead I asked, "Who stayed behind?"

"You already know the answer to that." Ken chuckled as he hung up.

"Me," came an ice-cold voice from behind.

Ken had been right; I did know the answer. And as I heard the ominous click of Ian loading a round into the chamber of an automatic pistol, I wondered whether the extra million I had been paid to betray my friends was really much of a bargain after all.

THE RISE OF THE ZOMBIE MORRIS DANCERS

This 28th of December, I did as I do every Holy Innocents Day, I locked my door and hid. Why? Because, some forty years ago, my malevolent headmaster – driven insane by his long years of imprisonment in the village where we both lived – tried to obtain his freedom by sacrificing me on an ancient stone altar. Even now he is still hunting me, seeking revenge for his failure to achieve his aims.

Each year, as Christmas approaches, my sleep becomes filled with nightmares of him lifting me onto the slab, while a dark witch, prehistoric stone knife held high, prepares to remove my heart. In my dreams, I struggle to evade his icy grasp, but there is no escape. My getaway is blocked by the menacing figures of the local morris dancers. And through all this, my father dithers over whether to save me, his only child.

It is only as the year turns that my dreams return to normal.

*

On the surface, at least, Episcopi Parva, or simply Parva, nestled deep within the Cotswold hills, is stunningly beautiful. With its ivy-clad, stone-built, thatched-roofed cottages, it is the spiritual home of elderly spinster detectives, country vets and the servants of the big house on the hill so loved by the writers of afternoon TV fiction. During the summer months, it is not unknown for four or five film crews to be visiting at the same time, queueing to capture their star performer entering the post office or tea rooms. On occasion, the logjam becomes so lengthy that violence ensues.

As the nights draw in and the cameras depart, however, things change. Parva, standing at the crossroads of disillusionment and despair, becomes as it has for over a thousand years: home to seething undercurrents of bitterness, jealousy and rage. The layers of hatred built up over generations are as much part of Parva's heritage as the age-blackened walls of the Norman church or the brooding moss-covered henge. Sitting at each end of the main street, they guard the village from intruders, or perhaps it is the other way around.

It was to here, a place I had never visited before, that I was exiled aged seven.

*

The afternoon my school in West London broke up at the end of summer term, I arrived home to be told that I would be spending my holidays in the village where my father had been born and raised. My mother had died a few months previously, and my father, struggling to keep his job and look after me, had agreed with his sister that she would take charge during the school holidays. It didn't turn out that way. Within days of me moving there, a cruel twist of fate changed everything. My father applied for and was hired for a job in the village. So, instead of going home at the end of the school holidays, my banishment became permanent.

Obviously, things had been difficult since my mother's death, but, with the help of a school I loved and a close circle of supportive friends, I had got through it. Now faced with the prospect of being separated from them forever, I was, as I thought, at the lowest point of my life. How wrong I was.

I soon discovered that along with the handicap of being an incomer, I was also related to the two most hated individuals in the village. The first – a man of courage, determination and fortitude – was my dad, or as everyone else knew him, the new village bobby. The second, a woman held responsible for every calamity that befell the community, my aunt. But that is the downside of being the resident witch I guess; you get blamed for every little thing that goes awry. As soon as my fellow pupils found out who I was, I was sniped at and bullied at every turn. Had everyone just ignored me, I think I could have coped. Just.

From the distance of all those years, I do have a little sympathy for the other children. For anyone growing up in Parva, the outlook is bleak. If you are a boy, the only real escape from a life of back-breaking farm labour, alcoholism or both is the army or prison. The girls, on the other hand, have no future beyond underaged pregnancy followed by an endless stream of snotty-nosed, scabby-kneed brats. You can understand why someone arriving from outside, bringing with them even the vaguest prospect of escape, was in their eyes damned. For the adults, there was no excuse. Other than Mr 'call me Jack' Green, the drink-addled church warden, they were without exception cruel and ignorant. You might have thought that they would have known better, but they did nothing to support a lonely grieving boy.

After the first few weeks, a period that lasted an eternity at my age, things did improve a little, however. My deliverance came courtesy of Baz and Jed, a couple of leather-clad teenagers – the sole members of the local heavy-metal band. When not practising at full volume in the church hall, they spent their days lounging around the village square midway between the church and the henge, drinking cheap cider and shouting abuse at any passer-by unfortunate enough to catch their eye. At first, they included me in their mockery, calling me names and stealing my lunch money.

They soon came to the attention of my father who, always on the lookout for a quiet life, made them an offer they couldn't refuse. In return for them promising not to make too much of a mess, break anything, harm anyone and occasionally give him a swig of their cider, he would pretend that they didn't exist. To show their good faith in the arrangement, they included me in the deal and proceeded to ignore me completely.

Their indifference helped my social life no end and it was not long before some of the other pupils tagged along with me on our way to and from school. By pretending to be my friends, they were also snubbed and allowed to keep their lunch money. While starting out as friendships of convenience, these soon turned into passable imitations of the real thing. So, in their own way and for their own reasons, everyone was reasonably content, if not happy.

Happy is not a word one could ever use to describe Parva. The only possible exceptions were my dad who, reverting to his childhood, embraced village life to the full and Mr Green, with his wide grin cutting across his heavily bearded, drink-reddened face. Despite this improvement, there was still one dark cloud on the horizon. It came in the form of the vindictive, wrathful, weasel-toothed village headmaster, Mr Herod. But as he treated everyone, adult and child alike, with the same icy contempt, his malign influence over me was somewhat diluted.

It was not long, however, before my fragile rapprochement with the village came close to collapse. Being a policeman was not, it seems, sufficient humiliation for my father who, with no thought for me, decided to bolster his reputation by joining the local morris dancers. To make matters worse, as one of the few men in the village with any sense of rhythm, he was immediately promoted to the position of fool, which entitled him to carry a partially inflated pig's bladder mounted on a stick. Beyond proud, he hung it on the living room wall, demonstrating its use to anyone unwise enough to visit. My aunt, less enthusiastic about both him and the bladder, was heard to mutter that playing the fool was something that didn't really take much effort on his part. As it turned out, I was worrying unduly. Much to my surprise, his new position did not make matters worse, it actually improved things, particularly with Baz and Jed. Now if I passed them on the street, as long as there was no one within sight, they would nod in my direction and on one occasion even muttered, "Alright!"

*

I had kept alive some hope that we would go home for Christmas. I still thought of London, with its shop windows full of treats, streets lit with coloured decorations and a tall, illuminated tree in the middle of Trafalgar Square, as home. London promised me a proper celebration. I was disappointed, however. My father decided that we should stay in the village throughout the festivities. Had it not been for the mysterious disappearance of Mr Herod early in December, there would have been no cheer whatsoever. Oh, that's not quite true. There was always Mr Green. Covered in mistletoe from head to toe, he wandered the streets delivering beer-fumed kisses to anyone not quick enough to escape his clutches. Other than him, it was obvious that Christmas in Parva was not a time for celebration.

The only good news was that late on Christmas Eve, it started to snow. The first flakes, slow and lazy, came about nine and were soon followed by something much heavier. It fell throughout the night so that by the next morning, I awoke to my first-ever white Christmas. The snow continued all day, so heavy that it was impossible to go outside. Angry and resentful, I spent my day sitting at the steamy windows of our cottage watching it fall.

Boxing Day, though, broke bright and clear and, marked by nothing more than the occasional fox trail, the snow was now more than a foot deep.

Getting dressed as fast as I could and ignoring shouts from my father to wrap up warm, I ran to the square. It was already littered with small groups building snow men of amazing variety. My increasingly accepted place in village life was further cemented when Baz and Jed invited me to join them in creating a surprisingly good snow imitation of Mr Herod. To complete the picture, albeit inaccurately, they placed an empty cider bottle to his lips and, as a final touch, added a small tinfoil crown. Taking it in turns, they bowed in mock veneration. Although I had no idea why, I joined in. Then, calling a truce in their endless war with the children, they condescended to join in a snowball fight.

We might have carried on all day had Mr Herod not suddenly reappeared. Furious at the sight of the Herodman, he snarled and kicked wildly in a deranged attempt to destroy it. Then, turning on me, he promised to make my life a misery for the rest of my school days. For some reason, in his eyes, I was solely to blame for the insult. Head bowed, I slunk away, returning home sad, wet and frozen. When I told my father and aunt about his threats, instead of getting any sympathy, I was ordered to write a letter of apology and was sent to bed early.

I never got around to writing that letter. Had I done so, my life might have worked out differently.

The snow continued all day on the twenty-seventh, but now a deep gloom pervaded the whole village. Whether it was down to Mr Herod's return, I have no idea, but I had no desire to venture outside. I wasn't alone. As far as I could see, no one else left their house either.

So, when Holy Innocents dawned cold and overcast, I was resigned to being trapped inside for yet another day. I had already read all my comics several times over and was coming to terms with the fact that I might just have to write that letter when my father arrived home early.

"We are going to church this evening," he announced. "Go and have a bath and put on your best clothes."

Attending church wasn't normal for us. In fact, we hadn't been once since moving to Parva. *Was this outbreak of religious mania part of a descent into madness first revealed by his morris dancing?* I wondered. The answer, as it turned out, was much simpler. There had been trouble earlier in the day and my father wanted to make sure things didn't get out of hand at the evening service. Apparently, the vicar had accused Baz and Jed of taking and drinking a bottle of communion wine. They had been rehearsing in the village hall when the supposed theft took place and, with suspicion immediately falling on them, my dad had been called. When interviewed, both had vociferously denied the slur on their good names. The lack of wine odours on their breath and Baz's declaration of, "Have you ever tasted communion wine? I mean…" convinced him of their innocence.

*

Just after dark, nearly every villager gathered at the henge. From there, Mr Green, dressed all in white, marched us down the main street towards the church.

The few streetlights in the village had been switched off and every one of us held a lighted candle to guide our way. As we walked in solemn procession, we sang hymns. These were not the carols I had sung in my old school. They were chants from another time; ancient, dark and mysterious. Never having heard sounds like this, the hairs on my neck stood to attention, and a shiver ran down my spine. There was something so right about them on this day and in this place. That Holy Innocents in Parva carried far more significance than Christmas was becoming obvious. It was not until later that night that I learnt just how much more.

To add to the magic of the evening, it started to snow and, with the flakes glistening and glittering in the light of the guttering candles, I began to enjoy the spectacle. That was until we got to the square. There, our path was blocked by Baz and Jed.

Dressed in their best leathers, amplifiers connected and, for Jed at least, guitar in hand, they stood directly in front of our path, looking prepared for trouble. At first Mr Green tried to ignore them, carrying on as if nothing was amiss. But when he was about eight feet away, and with no sign of either Baz or Jed moving aside, he slowed and came to a halt. Obediently all the villagers stopped behind him, keeping their distance. If I was expecting my father to get involved, I was mistaken. He stood as still as everyone else, just waiting.

In his slow swaggering style, which involved placing his thumbs in his belt loops, leaving the rest of his hands free and rocking from side to side as he went, Baz walked up to Mr Green. Not stopping until they were mere inches apart, the pair eyeballed each other and, at that moment, Jed began to play. This was not his normal fare of thrashed chords and loud distortion. This was gentle, melodic and tuneful, wistful even. It spoke of the old days and deep within me I felt a hunger grow, a longing for the times before recorded history, a yearning for things unseen, and beings as ancient as the surrounding hills themselves.

As the music wove its spell, Baz began to dance. Slowly at first, he waved his hands above his head. Legs kicking high, he picked up speed, leaping and gambolling in perfect time to Jed's playing. Mr Green stood motionless, until, at an unseen signal, he pulled a pair of pristine white handkerchiefs from his trouser pockets and joined Baz in the dance. Moving in flawless accord, the pair led us down to the church, the sound of Jed's guitar fading as we went. He strummed the final chord at the exact moment Baz and Mr Green arrived at the church door. Bowing deeply to each other, they walked inside, Baz allowing Mr Green to go first. Already there, greeting the congregants, was the vicar and, standing alone in the corner, pinch-faced and pale, Mr Herod. Wherever he had been, he had obviously not benefitted from much sunshine.

While Mr Green walked around the church greeting those villagers who were not part of the procession, mainly the elderly for whom the long walk down the hill was probably too much, Baz, now joined by Jed, approached Mr Herod. Standing close, they might have been guarding him from the rest of the village or perhaps it was the other way around. Even so, occasionally one of the more elderly parishioners approached and, with the slightest of bows, whispered, "Your Majesty."

Mr Herod in turn acknowledged their salutation with the briefest nod of his head.

The only person missing was my aunt, but, as you know, witches have an uneasy relationship with the church and, in my aunt's case, with everyone else as well. I understood why she might not have felt welcome.

What followed was a fairly normal evening service with hymns, readings and a sermon. I was uncomfortable, however. Although it was my first time inside the church, that was not the problem. What I had seen on my way through the lychgate and into the churchyard worried me. Carved on the ancient timbers, broad and beaming, half-covered with a bushy beard and surrounded by long curly hair formed from the moss growing on the wood, was a face I recognised. Indeed, its owner was standing only a few feet away, loudly leading the hymns in a powerful but tuneless baritone. The carving was of Mr Green.

*

As I was put to bed that night, I questioned my father.

"Have you seen the carving on the lychgate?"

He nodded.

"It's Mr Green, isn't it?"

"It certainly looks like him, yes."

"But it's nearly a thousand years old."

"True. I don't know what to say, except that when I was your age, Mr Green looked exactly as he does now."

"But how?"

"No idea. Best not think about it too much. If you really need to know though, you could try asking your aunt."

It has to be said that 'ask your aunt' was not much of an answer. Witches, as I later discovered, are not to be relied on, even ones in the family. But at that moment I was so intrigued that I decided to enquire anyway.

"Aunt."

"Yes, my dear."

"Mr Green."

She pursed her lips. It looked like she had just eaten a lemon. Eventually she asked, "What about him?"

"Is he really a thousand years old?"

She paused.

"Older. Older than the henge and as old as the hills."

"But how? Why? No one can live that long."

"Don't know how, but he is the spirit of village. It was built around him to protect the world from the evils that dwell here. That's why."

"What evils?"

"Go to sleep." There was an edge to her voice, so I did what I was told. Without another word, she walked out of the room.

After all I had experienced that evening, it is hardly surprising that I struggled to get off to sleep.

I must have dozed, because much later I vaguely heard the old clock downstairs chime eleven. Its message was confirmed only a few moments later by the dull clanging of the cracked bell in the church tower. Not long after that the front door creaked and, shutting it quietly behind them, someone left. The closing was done in the sort of way that attracts far more attention than doing it properly does. Now I was wide awake. My aunt had left just after I went to bed, so it couldn't be her. That left my father or a burglar. I was far less worried about it being a burglar – we had nothing – than I was about it being my dad. He was all I had.

*

I was four or five when the midnight knock came. Voices talking very low, my mother crying, rushing to dress and leaving the house soon after. While I pretended to sleep, a policewoman looked into my room and walked across to my bed to check on me. My deepest fears had been realised: my father was dead, killed protecting the world from criminals. Lying there, eyes jammed shut, sick with worry, I tried to imagine what life would be like without him. Overwhelmed and terrified to move, I wet the bed.

He was not dead as it turns out, he had just slipped on a frozen pavement and broken his shoulder. Nothing too serious. But from then on, my world filled with panic every time he was called away at night. Once my mother had gone, my fears only doubled. Without him, I would be an orphan. The word, having entered my brain, refused to leave and I imagined the cruel Dickensian workhouse I would be deported to. While I pictured my father's mangled body lying somewhere on the mean streets of Parva, I became aware of a muffled sound. It was almost the same as the one the villagers had made processing earlier. This time, while there was no singing, there was something else. Soft, just at the level of hearing, was the sound that a multitude of small bells might make if you tried to muffle them. Intrigued, I jumped out of bed and, wrapping my dressing gown around me, ran to the window.

Trudging through the snow along the main street, heading in the direction of the henge, were the morris dancers. Masked and dressed in black, rather than their normal white, they had tied dark cloth around their calves to silence the bells. Meanwhile, my father capered amongst them, occasionally striking a fellow dancer on their backside with his now-blackened pig's bladder. At some point over the last few days, he had painted it. The question was: how would he ever get it back to its natural colour?

Still at the head of the procession as he had been earlier, but now covered from head to foot in a costume of leaves, was Mr Green. At the tail, robed in red with white fur trimmings, was Mr Herod. At his heels, a slavering, red-eyed dog stalked and just behind, as though they were there to stop him from escaping, were Baz and Jed.

I should have been scared. Actually, I was terrified, but my curiosity overrode everything. For the last few days, I had felt that the village hid a secret. Now I knew it did, and this was my chance to uncover it. Leaping down the stairs three at a time, I put on my wellington boots and, placing the door on the latch so I could get back in, I slipped outside and followed the march into the night.

I had been right; the dancers were headed towards the henge. By keeping my distance, I remained unnoticed, except perhaps for Mr Herod's dog, which, occasionally sniffing the air, pawed at the ground, growling ominously. It must have been unsure though, because it did nothing to raise the alarm.

Arriving at the henge, the procession walked inside the circle and gathered around the weathered stone in its middle. This was something none of us village kids would ever do. Although we egged each other on, laughing at the absurd tales of children going inside never to return, we would never have taken the risk.

Next to the henge was a closely planted stand of yews. From the inside, I would get a clear view of the action while remaining invisible. I pushed my way in. At first the trees crowded in on me, until, without warning, they thinned, leaving an open space. There was no moon or stars inside; the trunks must be leaning in to form an enormous, vaulted roof. Unable to see clearly, I held out my arm and shuffled forward, until, after an age, I reached the other side. Like a Tardis, the stand was much bigger on the inside than out. Finding a gap, I pushed my way between two trunks until I had a clear view of the assembly.

As I watched, enthralled, the clouds parted and as the light from the moon glistened on the icy stone, I saw, standing behind it, a woman. Swathed in a dark cloak, she was carrying a huge stone knife. At that moment, Baz and Jed, grunting and sweating, arrived and lifted a squealing pig onto the altar. While it struggled to squirm free, they did their best to hold it still as the woman raised her knife to the sky. I turned away. I didn't want to see what was coming next. The presence of the pig did answer one question though. My father would not need to get the bladder repainted; he was going to have a brand-new one.

*

A growl by my ear and an iron-cold hand on my shoulder made me jump. I was no longer alone. While I hadn't wanted to see the pig die, I now looked out on something far, far worse. There, lips pulled back, yellow pointed teeth bared, bloodshot eyes staring wildly, his face contorted in rage, was Mr Herod. Digging his long, sharp nails deep enough to draw blood, he pulled me through the trees and dragged me into the circle. All the while, his dog snapped at my heels. By the time we reached the stone, I was squealing along with the pig.

"A spy," he hissed. "He must die."

A gasp came from the others.

"He is just a child," said Mr Green. "Don't you think you have killed enough of them already, Your Majesty?"

My father was silent, although his pig's bladder did sag a little.

"Look where your last slaughter got you," continued Mr Green. "Imprisoned here for eternity. Doomed to leave only once a year to deliver presents to those children you so despise. Must there be more deaths?"

"Those not invited can never know our secrets. It is the law. I repeat, he must die. And when he does, I shall be free," Herod answered.

"You will never be free," shouted Mr Green.

"Herod is correct," replied the woman with the knife. "The boy must die."

My fear was now replaced by a sheer cold terror. Beginning in my stomach, it spread through my body as I recognised the woman's voice. It was my aunt.

"Bring him to me," she commanded.

Showing surprising strength for someone so skinny, Herod pushed the pig from the table, allowing it to run, oinking and grateful, into the woods, and lifted me onto it. I was so frozen that when my aunt pushed me down flat and raised her knife, I offered no resistance. Looking into her blood-red eyes, the pupils showing nothing more than narrow catlike slits, I saw no sign of recognition and I prepared to die. Taking aim, my aunt closed her eyes and plunged the knife downwards. As it whistled directly towards my heart, a warm, soft hand pulled me from the stone. As I hit the mossy ground, the knife struck the stone and shattered. As it did, my aunt screamed – a sound that no human should ever be made to hear. At first, I thought my rescuer was my father, but, no, he was still frozen to the spot, watching the scene with unseeing eyes. Instead, I found myself staring into the rheumy gaze of a green-clad man.

"Quickly, lad," he ordered.

As I clambered up, he grabbed my hand and began to run.

"Come on, man, move," he screamed at my father.

Mr Green's words unfreezing the spell, my father shook his head clear and, finally realising what was going on, joined us in our sprint to freedom.

As we tumbled though the trees, I heard a crashing behind us and the sound of a panting dog. It was so close that I could feel its hot breath damp against my legs. By doubling my efforts, I managed to gain a few more inches. Then, with a squeal, the dog was no longer on my heels. Risking everything, I glanced back. Tail between its legs, it was slinking away, while Baz looked admiringly at his now bloodied DMs. Close by, Jed had wrestled Mr Herod to the ground and was holding him in a neck lock. All was not well though; the morris dancers were now involved in the chase, and they were getting closer by the second.

Arriving at our cottage, Mr Green bundled me into my dad's sidecar and, turning to the morris men, went on the attack. This bought enough time for my father to fire up his old Triumph combination and drive away, all three wheels sliding on the frozen cobbles. My last sight of the village was Baz and Jed waving goodbye, while Mr Green fought for his life, using his bells as nunchuks.

"Thank you," I called.

"No obligation," he replied, "but never come back." He still found enough time in the middle of his battle of life and death to give me the briefest of smiles.

I often wonder what became of Mr Green; I never saw him again. A stalwart of village life, did he become an outcast because of me, forced to live out the remainder of his life alone and shunned? Or is he, as I hope, still living a life of quiet contemplation, tending to the village church he so obviously cherished?

Looking back, I realise that I learnt three things that night. First, Parva seems to be some sort of prison for many of the ancient evils in the world. Far more than just Mr Herod, I think. I believe that Mr Green is their jailer, keeping them under lock and key by some form of primeval magic. In this, he is ably assisted by Baz and Jed as his warders. I now understand why the village is so unchangeable and so unhappy.

Second, it is not just Parva where such beings live. They are amongst us everywhere. While most do their best not to be too obvious, they are there if you care to look for them. Some are angels sent to protect us, others are the grey folk living as humans, while yet more are immortals doomed to spend eternity awaiting their destiny. Do you know I once met King Arthur at a party in North London? He was absolutely wasted at the time and wouldn't stop moaning about how sleeping with his half-sister had ruined his life. But that is another story, hopefully one I will get to at some point.

If you want to meet these people, all you need to do is to keep your eyes and mind open and soon you will recognise them for what they are. I have discovered that other than the Herods, they are mostly approachable and willing to talk freely about themselves. Always about themselves, I have noticed. It can get very tedious indeed. And why shouldn't they be open to talking to you? They are bored. They have been hanging around for hundreds of years pretending to be something they are not. Also, there is little danger to them. As immortals, they are, after all, fairly indestructible. Anyway, who would believe you if you started a conversation with, "Hey, have you met my new girlfriend? She's a two-thousand-year-old Irish goddess." You can see how that chat would go.

Oh, and that third thing; I simply had to learn to play and dance like Baz and Jed. I have never got to be as good as them though, but they have had a long time to perfect their craft.[1]

---

[1] Green Man, Jack in the Green or Robin Goodfellow type stories appear in many cultures, not just in the UK but also in Europe and as far afield as Asia. Some date back to the second century CE. That would make my Mr Green over eighteen hundred years old, older than the village church in Parva, although perhaps not as ancient as the henge. In most stories, the Green Man is a symbol of rebirth and the new growth of spring. That would fit quite nicely with my Mr Green and his place in the fabric of Parva. Whether there is just one Green Man or many, I have no idea, but I quite like the idea of my Mr Green being unique.

Obligations. You ought to know that saying thank you to one of the old or grey folk for any favour offered or accepted will place you under an obligation to return the said favour. I did not know this, but Mr Green obviously did and made it clear that I was not being placed under any obligation for thanking him for my rescue.

The association of Herod the Great from the Biblical Christmas stories with Father Christmas seems far more obscure and perhaps little more than wishful thinking on my part. However, it does seem fitting that the man who ordered the massacre of all the boy children in his kingdom, just to eliminate a perceived threat from the infant Jesus, should be punished for eternity. Being compelled to deliver presents to all the world's children seems an appropriate way of doing it. Although he does not specifically refer to Father Christmas, the imagery of Herod in Charles Causley's Innocents Song certainly makes me think of him as Santa and that was what I used as my inspiration.

Black Dog legends occur primarily in East Anglia, where there are many stories of a large, red-eyed dog (Black Shuck), who is the portent of death. Similar legends in the Cotswolds (where the fictional Parva is located) seem few and far between and much sketchier. However, every baddy needs a sidekick, and a Black Dog seems far more appropriate than a ravening reindeer under the circumstances.

Let me apologise unreservedly to any morris dancers I have offended. All those I have met and danced with have been as fine a group of gentlemen as you could ever wish to meet, albeit occasionally a little too fond of their beer. In case you are interested, the tune Jed plays and Mr Green and Baz dance to is the Gloucester Hornpipe. I can thoroughly recommend a listen. You can find it on most streaming services.

Finally, Baz and Jed are purely products of my imagination. They are the teens I would love to have been if only I had had the courage to act out my real personality.